I0714166

A PLACE CALL "THERE"

The Secret Place

DEBORA COLEMAN

Copyright @2021 by Debora Coleman

All rights reserved. No part of this book may be reproduced in any form or by any electronic or mechanical means, including information storage and retrieval systems, without permission in writing from the publisher, except by reviewers, who may quote brief passages in a review.

This publication contains the opinions and ideas of its author. It is intended to provide helpful and informative material on the subjects addressed in the publication. The author and publisher specifically disclaim all responsibility for any liability, loss or risk, personal or otherwise, which is incurred as a consequence, directly or indirectly, of the use and application of any of the contents of this book.

WORKBOOK PRESS LLC
187 E Warm Springs Rd,
Suite B285, Las Vegas, NV 89119, USA

Website: https://workbookpress.com/
Hotline: 1-888-818-4856
Email: admin@workbookpress.com

Ordering Information:
Quantity sales. Special discounts are available on quantity purchases by corporations, associations, and others.
For details, contact the publisher at the address above.

ISBN-13:   978-1-953839-87-9 (Paperback Version)
           978-1-953839-88-6 (Digital Version)

REV. DATE: 21/01/2021

Acknowledgements

My deepest appreciation to my husband, Robert, who challenged me in my calling did not allow me to be comfortable in where I was as a believer. You are truly a work of art.

To my five precious children. Adrien, Quetta, Shonda, Crystal, Sophia.

To my grands Makayla, Josie Christopher new addiction to the family, and my son-in-law Steve.

To my mother, who always encourage me even if she does not understand what I am doing until it is finished.

To my sisters and brothers that I took care of coming up I learn from you all; Bobby, Milford, Andrea(deceased), Jacqueline, Darien, Patrick, and Katrina a/k/a Big Drew.

To my deceased father Clifford Edward Jones.

Introduction

There is a place call there where we can go in God to get rest for our souls it is a place call there. When we go from one realm of the spirit from glory to glory we will find rest in the secret place of the Most high, for we will learn to live there in this special place call there; after going from place to place where and there I just know when you are burned out of the same church as usual, because spiritual journey go all the way to boredom . Come on this journey with me into the awesome supernatural place of the true and living God where you will never get bored.

Psalms91:1-16

He that dwell in the secret place of the Most high shall abide in the shadow of the Almighty.

I will say of the Lord, he is my refuge and my fortress: my God; in whom I trust.

Surely, he shall deliver thee from the snare of the fowler, and from the noisome pestilence.

He shall cover thee with his features, and under his wings shall thou trust his truth shall be thy shield and bucker.

Thou shall not be afraid for the terror by night, nor for the arrow that fiftieth by day.

A thousand shall fall at thy side, and ten thousand at thy right hand; but it shall not come nigh thee.

Only with thine eyes shalt thou behold and see the reward of the wicked.

Because thou hast made the Lord, which is my refuge, even the Most High thy habitation.

There shall no evil befall thee, neither shall any plague come nigh thy dwelling.

For he shall give his angels charge over thee, to keep thee in all thy ways.

They shall bear thee up in their hands, lest thou dash thy foot against a stone.

Thou shall tread upon the lion and the adder the young lion and the dragon shall thou trample under feet.

Because he hath set his love upon me, therefore will I deliver him; I will set him on high, because he hath known my name.

He shall call upon me, and I will answer him I will be with him in trouble, I will deliver him and honor him.

With long life will satisfy him and shew him my salvation.

A Place Call There

On this Journey to a place call there you will encounter many setbacks, disappointments, fears, rejection, but God will call you to the place he has for you in him and when you get there you will be in such awe for you will know you are in a place that you never been before it will wonderfully amaze you. How do this place call there starts? The place call there starts in pray not just any prayer, but effective prayer we are call to the threshing floor of prayer, not only prayer also praise and worship which is a form prayer I want to get the word out to let you know there is a place in God call there.

To start out on this journey to the place call there we are to get dressed there will be all out warfare when you make up your mind to really surrender unto God your reasonable service. Your mind will be transformed to serve the true and living God without compromise. Your family will not understand your friends will not understand and, will oppose you even the church will become unfamiliar place for the spiritual strongholds must come down. A spiritual stronghold is a place in the mind where there is an accumulation of thoughts that seem to give a good reason to sin. It can also, be a place in the thought system where wrong thinking have accumulated for years even, beginning while we were young. One writer said, a stronghold is extra strong when one believes a lie and argue against the truth; when strongholds come down pride comes down, we are to pull down the strongholds come down pride comes down we are to pull down the strongholds through prayer and the word, praise and worship.

Corinthians 10:4-6

For the weapons of our warfare are not carnal, but mighty through God to the pulling down of strongholds pulling down every imagination that exalt itself against the knowledge of God bringing every thought captive to the obedience of Christ. In getting dress the priest in the old testament priest put the MITRE upon his head also upon the MITRE even upon his forefront did he the golden plate the holy crown; as the Lord commanded Moses.

Exodus 28

36. *And thou shalt make a plate of pure gold and grave upon it, like the engravings of a signet, HOLINESS TO THE LORD.*

37. *And thou shalt put it on a blue lace, that it may be upon the forefront of the MITRE it shall be.*

38. *And it shall be upon Aaron forehead that Aaron may bear the iniquity of the holy things, which the children of Israel shall hallow in all their holy gifts: and it shall be*

always be upon his forehead that they may be accepted before the Lord.

On your journey to your place call there you must get dressed we are to pull down strongholds to build up the kingdom for everything that the Lord showed the old prophets to do and build is in the kingdom of Heaven we are bring heaven to earth so get dressed!

Zechariah 3:5

And I said, let them set a fair MITRE upon his head. They set a fair MITRE upon his head and clothed him with garments. And the angel of the Lord stood by.

Philippians 2-5

Let his mind be in you which was also in Christ Jesus. Who being in the form of God, thought it not robbery to be equal with God.

Fellowship with God

Learning to communicate with God in fellowship to come into his presence with; thanksgiving and praise learning to feel his presence, hear his voice, yes this is a learning experience on your way the place call there as you begin to let him purify you because, purification is necessary. Purification is necessary for the practical reason of true perception in your hearing words the way you will receive what you are hearing. God will need to purify the heart. It is part of processing God when the Word is perceived in our hearing. We need to perceive it right in the processing order so, when the word is heard the process is the purify you.

The enemy will come to attack the word that you hear this is the enemy assignment to come against the word that in you, because he hates the word Jesus is the living Word. If you get the word inside your heart and soul to apply it to your life it will change you to walk in victory. The process is important to the place call there, so you will soon learn to pray without ceasing.

1 Thessalonians 5:17-21

Pray without ceasing … In everything give thanks for, this is the will of God in Christ Jesus for you. Quench not the Spirit. Despise not prophesying. Prove all things; hold fast that which is good.

It is a lesson on practicing the presence of God even in praise and worship a journey of committee and devotion on your way to you place call there it is like a spiritual detox.

1. Detox your spiritual heart
2. Detox your spiritual eyes
3. Detox your spiritual ears
4. Detox your spiritual words
5. Detox your spiritual actions

Psalms 100

Make a joyful noise unto the Lord, all ye lands.

Serve the Lord with gladness it is he that hath made us, and not we ourselves; We are the people, and the sheep of his pasture. Enter- into his gates with thanksgiving and into his courts with praise: For the Lord is good; his mercy is everlasting; and his truth endure to all generations.

Praise is what I do even when I am going through on my way, I had to learn to praise God in the mist of my good and my bad all my trails and life circumstances, hurting to the point I know I just wanted to quit, and give up throw in the towel.

In February 2013 I lost my only grandson to a gunshot to the chest only seventeen years old, here I am a born- again believer in the church, saved and wash in the blood of the Lamb. I was hit with a certain trail out of my control. I received a call informing me my only grandson have been shot rush to the hospital fighting for his life. This was one of the most painful time in my life. Damarcus died February 22, 2013 around 2:30 a.m. I press my way through. The enemy was definitively on his job even though I was marked, talked about, persecuted; even by family members.

It is the time that you get closer to God not run away from him letting him go was unbearable What are you to do when your whole world is turned upside down in one night? It has been five years now since his death but, his memories of the good times I hold close to my heart. The Lord took me to the book of Job I truly believe this is when I had a paradigm shift. When I shifted from church tradition to a true relationship with Jesus Christ. It is time that you give him all the praise. Because the Lord giveth and the Lord taketh. This is a big test of faith.

Suffering

On this journey to a place call there is often call to a place of suffering you will need to die to the flesh. Now I am not saying you will become perfect in all your ways. I am saying, you will have a change come within you. Sometimes you will have to experience the word that is given to you by the LORD to walk it out in other words, live it. This is a love- faith journey so you will learn to live by faith and learn to forgive on your journey. You will not walk by what you see this will be a matter of the heart you will learn to trust God not the arms of the flesh. Jesus learn obedience through the things he suffered you will go through the suffering process too. God is more concerned about forming his character in you than; you to having a mighty ministry. The fellowship of his suffering will teach you a life lesson through the things you suffer. You will need to stand strong in the battle it will go from level to level every level is a different experience.

Repentance must be a way of life, be willing to pay the price in the school of life. God will retrain you for the   ministry and purpose where by which you were called. This journey to your place God will have to purify your character, and your gifts you will have go through the process to become and proven authentic the process will take you on a highway of holiness.

Isaiah: 35-8

And a highway shall be there and a way, and it shall be called: The way of holiness; the unclean shall not pass over it; but shall be for those: the wayfaring men, though fools; shall not err therein.

Once the Lord begin the process of sanctification and purification you will begin to have dreams, and visions where he will visit you during time of resting. This is when you begin to come into and be moved with awe, because you are headed in a direction that you never walked before. This journey is a word journey on the way to the place call there. It is not only learning to walk it out you want to learn how to apply the word to the circumstances and issues in your life. Learning the principles and the laws of his commandments.

Psalms 119-105

His word becomes a lamp unto my feet; and a light unto my path.

1 John 1:5

Walking in the light of God in him there is no darkness. Light is a metaphor of righteousness and goodness, then darkness signifies evil and sin. If we say we have fellowship with him yet walk in darkness, we lie and do not live out the truth. Walking in the light is walking in righteousness. That brings me to another piece of the garment which the priest wore.

The Breast Piece
Exodus 29:25-28

Fashion a breast piece for making decisions the work of skilled hands. Make it like the phoned: of gold, and blue, purple and scarlet yarn, and of finely twisted linen.

22. "For the breast piece make braided chains of pure gold, like rope.

23. Make two gold rings for it and fasten them two corners of the breast piece.

24. Fasten the two gold chains to the rings at the corners of the breast piece.

25. And the other ends of the chains to the two setting, attaching them to the shoulder pieces of the phoned at the front.

God promise the garment of praise for the spirit of heaviness when you take the focus off self and give him praise that is due him something change within. He is bigger than our problem; our circumstances; our situations. Let everything have breath praise the Lord. We don't praise because we feel like it, why? because praise is what I do it is a lifestyle. It is what I do even when I am going through as we put on the garment of praise, we focus on praise for it is one of the weapon against the strongholds that need to be cast down. We will walk in victory and power so let us offer him the sacrifice of praise to our God, that is the fruit of our lips, giving thanks to his name.

Hebrew 13:15

This means that we are to walk in a mold of praise continually covering ourselves with praise giving thanks to him in all things the good and the bad. What is praise? We praise God in songs, music, dance no matter how we express our praise to him. We must lift his name above every name for the Lord is great and greatly to be praise, he is to be feared with reverence of his Holy name. On your way to you place call there be sure to continually give him all the praise, and honor due him all the glory belongs to him. Praise is another form of warfare prayer to pull down strongholds in our life.

Praise the Lord! Praise God in his sanctuary
Praise him in his mighty firmament!
Praise him for his mighty acts;
Praise him according to his excellent greatness!
Praise him with the sound of the trumpet
Praise him with the flute and the Harp!
Praise him with the tambourine and dance;
Praise him with the stringed instruments and flutes!
Praise him with the Loud cymbals!
Praise him with the clashing cymbals!
Let everything that has breath praise the Lord.
Praise the LORD! *(Psalms 150:1-6)*
Let us take up the garment of praise for the spirit of heaviness our God in a God of true praise.

Worship is not the same as praise were worship is coming into intimacy with him praise is the preparation to take you into that intimacy with him. On your journey it becomes a way of life it is about adoration unto the King of Glory. We worship in spirit and in truth; being a royal priesthood unto the Lord we are called children of the light, to walk in the light. Jesus left us a comforter to lead and guide us into all his truth, you shall know the truth and the truth shall set you free, in your spirit, in your mind, in your heart without the indwelling of the Holy Spirit there is no revelation of truth. The journal to your place will call for true intimacy with him, brokenness, and transparent. He the Holy Spirit will become you friend to lead, guide, and come alone side you to help you the place of worship is an awesome wonderful place to be, but you will have to press in to the kingdom. If you are in a dry place your wilderness you will receive revelation of the Risen Christ, you will seek him with all your heart he will be found.

The Seven Spirits of God

There are Seven Spirits of God in this place you will discover that:
* Spirit of Justification
* Spirit of Sanctification
*Spirit of Truth
*Spirit of Wisdom
*Spirit of Deliverance
*Spirit of Prayer
     a.   This is the work of the Spirit of God *(1 Cor. 6:11)*.

b.   A process of Gods' grace by which the believer is separated from sin, purified by life lived in the Spirit. *(Roman 8:1-4)*

c.   For the of the Spirit of Life in Christ Jesus has made me free from the law of sin and death *(Romans 8:2)*. The Spirit of Truth whom the world cannot receive, because it neither sees him nor knows him, but you know him, for he dwells with you and will be in you.

d.   The Spirit of Wisdom- that the God of our Lord Jesus Christ the father of glory may give to you the Spirit of wisdom and revelation in the knowledge of him. *(Ephesians 1:17)*.

e.   The Spirit of deliverance-but if I cast out demons by the Spirit of god surely the kingdom of God has come upon me. It is by the power of the Holy Spirit that we are delivered from sin and by the same Spirit demons are cast out and the powers of darkness are defeated remember the gift is the gift of the Holy Spirit. The gifts don't belong to us to do as we please, but to work in the Kingdom of God can God trust us with his gifts? *(Matthew 12:28)*

f.   The Spirit of Prayer- Likewise the Spirit also helps our weakness, for we do not know what we should pray for as we ought, but the Spirit himself makes intercessions for us with groanings which cannot be uttered (Romans 8:26). On your journey the fruits of the Spirit will be developed what are these fruits that God is so concern with us bringing them forth in our life and character? These are the nine attributes of the person of Jesus Christ: But the fruit of the Spirit is love, Joy, peace, patience, kindness, goodness, faithfulness, gentleness, and self-control." A good tree cannot bear bad fruit, nor can a rotten tree bear good fruit. Every tree that does not bear good fruit will be cut down and thrown into the fire by their fruits you will know them. *(Matthew 7:17-20)*.

Love-and you must love the Lord your God with all your heart, all you soul, and strength and love thy neighbor as thy self: through his love he drew me, through his love he saved me, and delivered me the greatest of them all is love. *(Deuteronomy) 6:5*

1.   Peace- This flow like a river down in you it will quite your soul with such tranquility. May the Lord show favor toward you and give you peace. (Numbers 6:26)

2.   Faithfulness- great is thy faithfulness our God is faithful even when we are not faithful, but he wants us to learn to be faithful in all that we do and to him and toward others. *(Lamentations 3:23)*.

3.   Joy- I get Joy when I think about all that he has done for me how he set me free, delivered from the kingdom of darkness into his marvelous light I get joy, joy, joy.

4.   Goodness- O taste and see that the Lord is good like honey in

a rock. Have you ever tasted how sweet honey is? He is like honey in a rock his goodness shall last through all generations. *(Psalms 23:6).*

5.	Gentleness- He is such a gentleman; not pushy if forceful just lead, and guide with quietness. He is a gentleman.

6.	Patience- to me patient is one of the hardest fruits to developed, but God is patient with us he will test your patient and faith if you pass the test you will do well but if, not you will have to take it over until passed.

7.	Self -control – This fruit comes through much prayer and reading of the scriptures the flesh will have to die.

8.	Kindness- This fruit is not very hard to develop if you are already kind to others, or that was your up- bringing it will remain.

When we follow and obey the spirit's lead instead of being led by the flesh; or our self-focus desires, he the Spirit will produce in you the fruits of God by yielding unto him daily.

We are a Royal Priesthood

On your journey to the place call there all believers in Christ are called priest and kings unto God and we need to get dress properly to meet him in the Holy of Holies. The priest in the Levitical priesthood had to come in dress for service unto the Lord. The priest dressed in long robes of blue golden bells were attached to the hem and pomegranates made from materials hung between the bells these pomegranates represents the fruits of the Spirit, and the bells represents the gifts of the Spirit. In my book the interpretation of dreams I talked you will keep moving toward you place. Signify that the gifts and fruits go together. The is a place in God where we can go the enemy voice becomes silent, but we must get dressed we are priest and kings unto God separated set apart for his service unto the Lord.

"Aaron and his sons must wear the garments whenever they were to enter the tent meeting or approach the altar to minister in the Holy Place, so that they will not incur guilt or die."

Exodus 28:43

There is first and foremost Prayer, Praise and Worship now that you are dressed for service to continue the journey you may enter his gates with thanksgiving and praise. Upon entering his gates, you must become a living sacrifice meaning you will have to die to the flesh. you may have a dream of getting shot or blood in the dream it will be the LORD dealing with your flesh. If you will not kill the flesh you can offer up strange fire unto the LORD. Surrender all unto him hold nothing back it is easy said than done. Aaron the high priest had two sons, Nadab and Abihu come in to offer incense with fire of their own without taking fire from the altar the LORD instructed.

What is strange fire? It is the flesh mixed with the Spirit calling it prayer, but the flesh is in war with the Spirit, no flesh shall glory in his sight. Nadab and Abihu were killed struck down dead by God. *(Leviticus 9:12)*

The Brazen Altar

The Instruction God gave Moses to make the brazen altar is where the animals were slain. Atoning the blood was poured or sprinkled for sin offering. The same altar is in heaven in the throne room where God dwells. He gave Moses specific instructions on how to make the altar in the tabernacle in the wilderness we are living epistle.

I Beseech you therefore my brethren by the mercies of God, that you present your bodies a living sacrifice, holy acceptable unto God which is your reasonable service. And be not conform to this world: but be you transformed by the renewing of your mind, that you may prove what is that good, and accepted, and perfect, will of God.

A call to the ministry to serve and minister unto the LORD serving the Lord with gladness of heart; learning to love God; learning to be obedient unto him and, learning to love and serve his people Coming to the brazen altar were the flesh is burned and put to death, this is what it is meant for the spiritual believers under the new covenant.

The Blood is Required

You will be required to apply the blood of Jesus without the shedding of blood there is no remission of sin. Jesus is the only way to the place called there the precious blood is a requirement there is not short cut, for he has redeemed us by his blood. We are bought with a price our righteousness in found in him alone. The blood of Jesus will never lose its' power. We can enter his presence through the shed blood of Jesus. The blood has always been a requirement. There is no more sacrifice of animals for the atonement for sin. Moses had spoken every perception to all the people according to the law. He took the blood of calves, and of goa with water, and scarlet wool and hyssop, and sprinkled both the book, and all the people, saying this is the blood of the testament which God had enjoined unto you moreover he sprinkled with blood both the tabernacle, and all the vessels of the ministry.

And almost all things are by the law purged with blood; and without the shedding of blood is no remission (forgiveness) of sin. It was therefore necessary that this pattern of things in the heavens should be purified with these; but the heavenly things themselves with better sacrifice than these.

Hebrew 9:19-24

It is through the redeeming blood of Jesus that is required on your way to the place call there every level the blood is required. He is called the Lamb of God; he is the perfect sacrifice. Now we can come boldly to the throne of grace through his shed blood.

Refiner's Fire

Now comes the fire to purify to prepare, equip for ministry the Lord calls and anoint his servants for ministry by taking you through the fire to purify your hearts he is a God of the heart for man looks on the outer appearance, but God looks on or in the heart. Therefore, the process is so important to be ready for his service in ministry you will have to surrender all let go and let God. He makes his ministry a flame of fire he is a God of fire.

Purification is necessary for the practical reason of the true perception of what you will be receiving from the Lord such as a word, a revelation perceiving what you are heating. Those strongholds of wrong deception must come down; for purification need to be a purifying of the heart and soul it is a matter of processing. When the word goes in our hearing perception, we can't be off you have to perceive it in its' right order line upon line precept upon precept; here a little; there a little.

Behold, I will send my messenger, and he shall prepare the way before me; and the Lord whom you seek, shall suddenly come to his temple, even the messenger of the covenant, whom you delight in: behold, he shall come, said the Lord of host.

But who may abide the day of his coming? And who shall stand when he appears? for he is like a refiners' fire, and like fullers' soap:

And he shall sit as a refiner and purifier of and he shall purifier of silver: and he shall purify the sons of Levi, and purge them as gold and silver, that they may offer unto the Lord an offering in righteousness.

Malachi 3:1-3

The Angel of Fire

In a burning bush while the bush was burning the scripture declare the bush was not consumed (burned up) a voice speaks from the bush is the voice of God speaking to Moses. In the realm of angels there are those that are call seraphim angels these are the angels of fire. These angels are said to have six wings they are flaming fire angels who comes with the fire of God. He calls Moses to the burning bush God is a God of fire

Elijah call fire down from heaven to consume Baal Idol.

Jeremiah declares it is like fire shut up in my bone, John the Baptist said, "He shall baptize you with the Holy Ghost and fire. The fire of God will burn out everything that is not like God the fire is a symbol of the presence of God. we see his presence, his passion and his purity, his fire is a purifier.

Luke 24:32

They said to each other, "Did not our hearts burn within us while he talked to us on the road, while he opened to us the scriptures.

Time to Wash

On your way to the place called there you will have to be washed with the water of the Word after the sacrifice, it is to go into service as a serving priest. The Priest had to wash at the laver altar. There is the blood and the water for washing and cleanse at the brazen altar points to the death of Jesus the brazen laver altar points to the life of Jesus Christ. Blood speaks of a life taken and water speaks of a life given.

You are clean through the word which I have spoken to you. *John 15:3*

He who believes on me as the scripture has said, out of you belly(heart) shall flow rivers of living waters.

John

And there is three that bear witness in earth, the Spirit, and water, and the blood: and these three agree is one 1 John 5:8

The Father, the Word, and the Spirit

What an awesome God we serve! He loves us with unconditional love, he gives us the living active Word that was made flesh even now, to wash away all sin and unrighteousness. Whenever we read the scriptures the Logos. We are washed with the water of the Word become clean for that day, or if we hear the Word through preaching and teaching. The water, the Word and the Holy Spirit all in agreement bearing record in the earth. The bible called them witnesses.

For these three bears a record in Heaven the Father, the Word(son) and the Holy Spirit: and these, three bear records in Heaven and these three are one. 1 John 5:7

1. *The" Father of lights" he is the light that shine in darkness in him there is no darkness. We are the sons and daughters of lights. Let your light shine so men can see your good works. He wants our light to be so bright even the devil will be blinded. Ask the Lord to give you a revelation on how bright the light is to see for looking upon.*

2. *Son he is the image of the invisible God, the firstborn of all creation*

the word made flesh.
   3.   *Holy Spirit is a mystery he is the breath of God he is the Spirit of God.*

In the beginning God said, "Let us make man in our own image in our likeness , after our own kind which is Spirit, God is a Spirit, so when we are regenerated, (born again) the Spirit is reborn then have to grow spiritually, then Jesus comes to take up resident inside he is the Word (seed) planted to grow into a big healthy tree. From there Jesus baptize you with the Holy Ghost (Spirit) and fire. There we have its father, son and Spirit functionalities are different they are the three who record in heaven.

The Man in the Mirror

The Bronze Laver was made from bronze mirror of the women it was at the bronze laver the priests wash their hands, and feet before entering; into the holy place. Therefore, as a priest unto God you must submit to the washing and cleansing for the ministry that god is preparing you for in that place call there. No Priest could enter the Holy Place with any trace of uncleanness. He must have clean hand and a pure heart to be in the service of the LORD. When you investigate the perfect law of God you are looking in the mirror at yourself, situation, issues, problems, circumstances. Seeing your true self for who you really are we find that mirror in the book of James where he talks about the mirror the Lord will show you self. Do not merely listen to the Word and deceive yourselves.

Do what it says, anyone who listens to the Word but does not do what it says is like a man who looks at his face in a mirror and, after looking at himself, goes away and immediately forgets what he looks like. But whosoever intently not do the perfect law that gives freedom, and continues in forgetting what they have heard, but doing they will be blessed in what they do." James 1:22-25 Read it, study, memorize, and do.

This book of the Law shall not depart out of your mouth, but you shall mediate in it day and night then shall thy make your way prosper than shall you have good success.

Joshua 1:8

As I have stated earlier everything God instructed his leader to do in the old testament is the pattern (shadow type) of what is in Heaven the Kingdom of Heaven have come to us in the form of apostolic-prophetic the kingdom is within it is time to walk in the kingdom to bring the kingdom of heaven to the earth realm. Washing in the bronze laver is symbolic for repentance; and water baptism this was introduce as Jesus come to be baptize by John the Baptist even though Jesus had no sin, he was a model for us. Jesus is our high priest who make intercession for us.

John the baptize prepared the way of the Lord; make his paths straight John came baptizing in the wilderness and preaching a baptism of repentance for the remission of sins. Then all land of Judea, and those from Jerusalem, went out to him and were all baptized by him in the Jordan River, confessing their sins.

Mark 1:1-5

Now Comes Revelation

Now comes revelation on your way to you place call there you will begin to get revelation after revelation comes wisdom and knowledge and understanding of the knowledge of Jesus Christ. God gave bronze Laver and instructed to Moses to make a lampstand in the tabernacle. The Priest can see have light in the Holy Place. This is another prophetic pattern from the Kingdom of Heaven a shadow type it was the Prophet Zachariah who saw the candlestick, or lampstand in heaven vision. This light is symbolic to revelation that is revealed unto us.

Zachariah 4:1-14

Zachariah vision of what he saw in heaven when the heavens open are if you are under an open heaven you will see vision and dream, dreams all the time.

And the angel who talked with me came again and woke me like a man who is awakened his sleep. And he said; to me "What do you see?" I said, "I see and behold a lampstand on it, with seven lips on ache of the lamps that are on the top of it. And there are two olive trees by it, one on the right of the bowl and the other on its left. "And I said to the angel who talked with me, answered and said to me, "Do you not know what these are?" said, "No my Lord."

Oil in the Lamp

You are the light of the world. A city set on a hill cannot be hidden *(Matthew 5:14)*.

Oil is often used as a symbol of the Holy Spirit who leads and guides us into all of God truths. If we look at the lampstand that was in the tabernacle the oil in the lamp represents being set apart equip for ministry. The oil of the Holy Spirit will flow through you when God's heart touches someone else heart. You are the tabernacle of God is with man. The oil flows as a river of love from the throne of grace. The Oil of the Lampstand symbolize your body the temple of the Holy Ghost you will need to learn to flow in the anointing of the Holy Ghost(Spirit). Learning to flow your body as the vessel that the oil flow through, become a vessel of honor you will have to be hungry for the oil to flow this is where you walk becomes a love walk.

I ask the Lord a question concerning the anointing wen like this: How do we flow in the anointing? The Lord said, "You have to flow in love and obedient. Jesus was not only obedient to his father, he also flowed in the anointing, for God anointed Jesus with the Holy Ghost. God empower his minister for the work of the ministry endowed with power from on high.

The Spirit of the Lord is upon me, because he has anointed me to preach the gospel to the poor. He has sent to proclaim freedom for the prisoners and recovery of sight for the blind, to set the oppressed free.

Luke 4:18

The Oil represents the presence of God in our life. It could be taken as the presence of the Holy Spirit. It's the oil in the lamp that keeps the fire burning. Which means there is a price to pay for the anointing, but it also means revelation that the Holy Spirit reveals to you concerning the things of God. To have a continual presence of God in our life we are to pay a price, by spending time at the feet of Jesus we need fresh oil in the body of Christ. The oil has been lost if we don't get the oil back, we are in trouble remember the strange fire with Aaron sons Na 'bad and Abihu took their censer, and put fire therein, and put incense thereon, and offered strange fire before the Lord, which he commanded them not. And there went out fire from the LORD, and devoured them, and they died before the LORD.

Leviticus 10:1-2

Even though the lampstand that burns the oil that gives us revelation in the Holy Place it is the Altar of Incense in the Holy Place were the prayers were offer unto God right before the priest went behind the curtains (veil). If we offer strange fire which is the flesh mixed with the Spirit, then how can we enter in? God is a Spirit he that worship him must worship in Spirit and Truth if not we will offer up strange fire in the Holy Place. When we offer up strange fire:
    1.   *We draw attention to ourselves, recognition, admiration.*
    2.   *Duplicating what God did. Where did that come from? Yes, the devil duplicates everything God does.*
    3.   *The fire was strange because everything that is in heaven where God is it*

is a pattern, a shadow type.

The censer full of burning coals of fire from off the altar before the LORD, are the shadow type from heaven the angels took the coals and touch the prophet lips come on stay with me now.

Isaiah 6:6

Then another of the seraphim flew to me with burning coal in his hand, which he had taken from the altar with tongs.

> 1. *He touched my mouth with it and sad, "Behold, this has touched your lips; and your iniquity is taken away and your sin is forgiven.*

Revelation 8:3

Then another angel, who had a golden censer, came and stood at the altar. He was given much incense to offer, along with the prayers of all the saints, on the golden altar before the throne.

Numbers 16:46

Moses said to Aaron, "Take your censer and put in it fire from the altar, and lay incense on it; then bring it quickly to the congregation and make atonement for them, for wrath has gone forth from the LORD, the plague has begun!"

Ezekiel 10:2

And he spoke to the man clothed in linen and said, "Enter between the whirling wheels under the cherubim and fill your hands with coals of fire from between the cherubim and scatter them over the city." And he entered in might sight.

What are you seeing?

I always say, it is only in Jesus that we know who we are." Paul prayed that the eyes of our understanding be enlightened and, that you know what the hope of his calling is and what the riches of the glory of his inheritance in the saints. And what is the exceeding greatness of his power toward us who believe, according to the working of his mighty power.

Ephesians 1:18-19

What are you seeing in the spiritual realm? Because you could be an eye in the body of Christ the eye is the Lamp of the body. If your eye is healthy, your whole body will be full of light, but if your eye is bad your whole body will be full of darkness.

Matthew 6:19-24

On your way to that place called there you will begin to see spiritually things you have never seen before it is like the bind eyes begin to see into the spirit realm your eyes are opening to the real world in the spiritual world. Just as your natural body have the eye is the sensory organs in the body the eyes are the ability to see in the bright and dim light. What are we eternal? What are you seeing in the body of Christ. Jesus use the term "This is my body." The body of Christ refers to members in the body, his body we are in him. Made up of those who have accepted Jesus Christ as their personal savior, baptized by one spirit into one body. I want to encourage you to not lose sight or give- up your testimony, for your testimony is a weapon. But Deborah the church takes my testimony, and use it against me, I still say do not give up your testimony! The Blood of Jesus still works it will never, never loose it's power. Jesus id the ultimate sacrifice he went to the Holies of Holies one time, for you and me our testimony is to help someone else.

Hebrew 9:12

Neither by the blood of goats and calves, but by his own blood he entered in once into the holy place, having obtained eternal redemption for us.

13. for the blood of bulls and of goats, and the ashes of heifer sprinkling the unclean, sanctification to the purifying of the flesh.

14. How much more shall the blood of Christ, who through the eternal Spirit offered himself without spot to God, purge your conscience from dead works to serve the living God?

You are part of the body, so it is your responsibility to find out if you are an eye. One reason why we should be part of a church body is to fulfill your calling to serve other believer in practical ways. The LORD uses a natural body and, parts to get his point across if one part fail to function you get sick. It is the same way in the spirit in the body of Christ body get sick.

What are you hearing?

Are you an ear in his body? You a vital part of the body of Christ, therefore we need truth that is to separate between the body of Christ, and these religious church building. Oh! LORD there you go getting me in trouble again speaking about the big deception. And I will say it still goes back to Jesus without him we would not know who we truly are in him. You may be asking, Deborah why is there so much competition, fighting for position? I say, to you that people don't know who they are in Christ, and there are tares in the Churches (buildings). If you are in him what you must do is to know that one else can do it but you.

There are many different people with their unique personality, and many different roles. Just as God have arranged the parts of the human body in correct positions. God has put the eyes, ears, arms, legs and son on the human body, he has also done it with the spiritual body. Joining together on one accord in unity the body would survive and maximize their potentials and gifting. Christians should not be jealous, inferior, haughty, or independent. My prayer is that we get it together, before return; until you have done what he, have call you to do he will not hold it against you ever.

Expect Persecution

On this journey to the place called there you will be persecuted for his name sake, it is a prophecy of Jesus who is giver of prophecies. If you have a personal relationship with him, and not playing church you will be persecuted for being real to the cause. Whatever he, have called you to do everyone will not agree or understand in following him there is a price to pay. What do you do in times to persecution? Well, I am glad you ask. Lets' investigate the old and the new testament. The life of Joseph the son of Jacob had prophetic dreams from God, he told the dream to his brothers the scripture declared his brothers were jealous, because of his dreams. Now I don't think Joseph ever dreamed literally that he would have to go to the PIT (Prophet in Training).

Genesis 37:23-29

And it came to pass when Joseph was come unto his brethren, that they stripped Joseph out of his coat, his coat of many colors that was on him;

24. And they took him and cast him into a pit: and the pit was empty, there was no water in it.

25. And they sat down to eat bread: and they lifted their eyes and looked, and behold, a company of Israelite came from Gilead with their camels bearing Spices

to carry it down to Egypt.

26. And Judah said unto his brethren, what profit is it if we kill our brother, and conceal his blood?

27. Come, and let us sell him to the Ishmaelites, and let not our hand be upon him; for he is our brother, and our blood and his brethren were content.

28. Then there passed by Midianites merchantman, and they drew and lifted Joseph to the Establishment for twenty pieces of silver and they bought Joseph into Egypt.

29. And Reuben returned unto the pit; and behold, Joseph was not in the pit; and he rent his clothes.

What? His dream did not come to pass away, so If you are in the pit you are on schedule, they stripped him of his clothes. This is a picture of Christ go to the cross, being persecuted by his own, scripture say he come to his own, and they received him not. If you survive in the pit it is like being in prison locked up, but don't give up you have to go through the refiner's fire. This is not the devil this is God taking you through training and preparation in the church (pit). Your pit experience doesn't have to have the favor of people to work and operate. Once you go through you will come out as pure Gold, because it is your faith that is being tested. God will get the glory out of this, for he will not share his glory with no one. We need to learn to discern between God and the devil, we have been taught that everything is of the devil; if we are going through life troubles, those who live a godly life shall suffer persecution. A real vision got to have a pit experience, for this is one of the way God works in and through you. I am writing from pit experiences praise Jesus!

Jesus was Persecuted

I want to use the betrayal of Judas Iscariot against Jesus because, Jesus was highly persecuted by many even his own. I want to use this scene because, most us go through betrayal and persecution by those who are close to us even those in our own household. We know Judas walk with Jesus for three and half years as the other, disciples but he betrayed Jesus with a kiss instead of just pointing him out he kissed Jesus on the cheek to sell him out. He threw a rock and put his hand behind his back. There are people close to us and live around us even in the church that persecute the Jesus in the inside because some people pretend to know him but, their actions show something different. Jesus already knew Judas would betray him the LORD will show you too who is for you and who is not because, they will resist the Spirit of God that is within you for no reason known.

Matthew26:21

"Truly, I say to you, one of you will betray me."
In Christendom there is always plotting this I have experience, but I say you have the love of the Father in you. How can you hurt of offend your sister, or brother in Christ intentionally? The answer to that question is one can and will not. It is the fake and false that does this, see Judas was not real, because how can one walk with the real, and not get it?

Matthew 5:10-12

Blessed are they which are persecuted for righteousness sake: For theirs is the Kingdom of heavens;
Blessed are you when men shall revile you and persecute you; and shall say all manner of evil against you falsely, for my sake, Rejoice, and be exceeding glad: for great is your reward in heaven: for so persecuted they the prophets which were before you.

Chronicles 7:14-15

If my people, who are called by my name, shall humble themselves, and pray, and seek my face, and turn from their wicked ways, then will I hear from heaven, and forgive their sin, and heal their land.
>   15. Now mine eyes shall be open, and mine ears attentive unto the prayer that is made in this place.

Matthew 7:11

If you then, being evil, know how to give good gifts unto your children, how much more shall your father which in heaven give good things to them that ask him? Now why did Jesus have to say, you being evil? Why couldn't he just say, now you being a child of God? Or you being a child of the king? Jesus called his people evil doers. Wow! There is nothing new under the sun the scriptures are an example of the hearts of men who without Jesus, and the Spirit of god will, and can't change. It is an inside job. We can dress up all we want to at the end of this life there will be a judge who sits high and looks low every man will be judged of himself. On your way to the place called there you will go through some dry places (desserts), pain, rejection, persecution, betrayal, it is all for the glory of God. He will make your feet like hinds' feet to walk in high places. He will plant you as a tree planted by the rivers of living waters. There will be obstacles and setbacks, but through them all you will learn lessons in the school of the hard knocks with the help of your helper (Holy Spirit).

God is a God of the heart, for he searches our hearts and mind I believe therefore King David was a man after Gods' own heart, David stayed in a mold of repentance, confessing, asking the LORD was I wrong? Search my heart if you find anything that is not pleasing to you LORD remove it far away from me. We learn who God is through our trails and error David a man after Gods' own heart.

1 Chronicles 28:9

As for you my son Solomon know the God of your father and serve him with a loyal heart, and with a willing mind: for God searches all hearts and understand all the imaginations of the thoughts: If thou seek him, he will be found of the: but if thou forsake him, he will cast thee off forever.

Wisdom from above

On your journey, after the persecution comes wisdom and revelation from above if you stay in sync, after every battle there is victory. The LORD your God will begin to visit you nightly, and you will fall in love with his presence. He will begin to captivate you and you will begin to be a God chaser, pursuing him day and night. He will become the lover of your soul in other words you are growing to maturity in your faith. *Chronicles 1:7*

In that night did God appear unto Solomon, and said unto him, what shall I give thee?

And Solomon said unto God thou hast showed great mercy unto David my father, and hast made me to reign in his stead.

Now, O LORD God, let thy promise unto David my father be established: for thou hast made me king over people like the dust of the earth in multitude.

Give me now wisdom and knowledge that I may go out and come in before this people: for who can judge this thy people, that is great?

And God said to Solomon, because this was in thine heart and thou hast not asked riches, wealth, or honor, nor the life of thine enemies, neither yet hast asked long life; but hast asked wisdom and knowledge for thyself, that thou may judge my people, over whom I have made thee king:

Wisdom and Knowledge is granted unto thee; and I will give thee riches, and wealth, and honor, such as none of the kings have had that have been before you, neither shall there any after you have this life.

Now this is what you call favor of the LORD when God visits you and tell you what you ask for was; not a selfish desire. You ask for my will not your will I am going to give you knowledge to know, and wisdom to apply what you know. Solomon was the son of King David. Solomon was his father successor, became the third and last king of the United Kingdom of Israel, following Ling Saul and his father King David. God gave Solomon the wisdom he even wrote the Song of Solomon, the book of Ecclesiastes, and Proverbs which is the book of wisdom after reading the first chapter of Ecclesiastes King Solomon, said, all is vanity, all his labor with his hand, his house, garden, planting he quotes:

18. Yea, I hate all my labor which I had taken under the sun: because I should leave it unto the man that shall be after me.

And who knows whether he shall be wise man or a fool? Yet he has rule over all my labor wherein I have labored, and wherein I showed myself wise under the sun. this is also vanity (empty).

In a nutshell only; what we do for Christ will last. Therefore, my prayer is Lord; not my will, but your will be done in my life, and in the earth realm. I don't want to be doing nothing I haven't been purposed or called to do. God will equip us to accomplish the tasks he calls us to do if we trust him and seek him with all our heart. Looking at King Solomon life a good start is not always a good finish. Wives that lead him into idolatry seven hundred wives, and three hundred concubines. Some of them were non-Jewish wives it behooves us to be very careful of the company we keep, those closet to us will affect our spiritual lives. Also, life lived apart from God will be meaningless, regardless of education, fulfilled goals, pleasure, abundance and wealth.

In the dispensation in the old testament Jesus had not come and ascend so it is by faith in God Solomon was justified for him to marry non-Jewish women, that didn't believe in the God of his fathers was considered unequally yoked together. Solomon marital decisions were direct violation of Gods' Law there is always consequences to the wrong decisions made. When writing a nonfiction, one is usually writing from experience, of the decision. All good thing comes from above, there is not a lot of opposition involved.

James 1:17-18

Every good gift and perfect gift is from above, and come down from the Father of lights, with whom is no variable, neither shadow of turning.

Now is the dispensation of the Holy Ghost, we have the power to walk right, talk right, live right, he will keep you if you want to be kept. Solomon did not have the promise of the Father, but he had the faith, wisdom, and revelation. These are examples for us, because someone lived it. The power of the Holy Ghost (Spirit) is the third person in the Godhead, he is the Spirit of the living God, was promised and, prophesy to come and reside inside the believer. He is the comforter that will comfort you in your hard times, and times of troubles these things I have spoken to you, that you should not be offend they shall put you out of the synagogues (churches); yea, the time come, that whosoever kill you will think that he do God service. And these things will they do unto you, because they have not known the father nor know me the Counselor.

He is the counselor the advocate he encourages he is the representative of Jesus Christ, he is the Spirit of Christ, he is our helper to lead and guides into all of God truth. He empowers us to accomplish the task he gives us. For it is the Spirit that reveals the truth of God. I always tell people; "I am in love with a man I have never seen". He walks with me, talks with me tell me I am his own. In his counseling he will convict the believer of sin to get rid of the things that are not pleasing to God. The Spirit works through our conscience to make us aware of our sin in our life. This is one of the works of the Holy Spirit therefore on your way to the place called there it is important to learn to listen to the voice of God, through his Spirit. Everything may not be sin, but it may be a weight, so we are to lay aside every weight, and the sin which so easily beset us. If we are carrying weight, baggage we are unable to run the race that is set before us. If we are in sin missing the, mark then we are in disobedience. How can we run the race? How can we obey the voice of God? Now we are missing the mark this is all about coming into maturity on your way to the place called there. This will require self-control and patience, so he will put you in the fire, and take you out the fire like to make you purify as pure gold.

The Holy Spirit Exalts Jesus

It is always the Spirit's mission to exalt Jesus the Spirit has come that we might be deeply impressed with the person of Jesus Christ. We are excited about his work. The purpose of the Holy Spirit is to exalt Jesus and lift him up. If we open our month and lift him up, he will draw all men unto him.

1. The Holy Spirit prompts us to worship.
    The time to be quiet in the presence of the Lord, a time to hear the word of the Lord: Be still and know that I am God" (Psalms 43:10). There is also a time to praise the Lord with upraised voice.
2. The Holy Spirit empowers up to worship.
    He empowers, equip us to witness, to tell about the goodness of Jesus, to give a solid testimony.
3. He gives us higher in the Spirit realm.

4.   The Holy Spirit helps us understand and apply what we learn because Jesus is the living Word, we are inspired by scriptures to take the scriptures apply it and live or walk it out.

John 1:1 .
2Timothy 3:16

All scripture is given by inspiration of God, is profitable for doctrine, for reproof, correction, rebuke.

Revelation 19:12

His eyes were as flames of fire, and on his head were many crowns; and he had a name written, that no man knew, but he himself. And he was clothed with a clothing dipped in blood: and his name is called THE WORD OF GOD. S no man knew his name, only who are led by the spirit of God knows that Jesus is the Living Word.

Revelation 1:2

Who bore record of the Word of God, and of the testimony of Jesus Christ, and all things that he saw.

Matthew 4:4

But he answered and said, it is written, man shall not live by bread alone, but by every word that proceed out of the mouth of God. The bible is profitable for us only if we are led by the Spirit of God, and one thing is needful that Jesus say our fellow ship with Jesus and to set down at his feet and listen, just as Mary the sister of Martha.

Learning to Flow

Luke 4:18

The Spirit of the Lord is upon me, because he has anointed me to preach the gospel to the poor; he has sent me to heal the brokenhearted, to preach deliverance to the captives, and recovering of sight to the blind, to set at liberty those that are bruised.

If the Lord has called you to do the work, he has given you the power of the anointing to flow, and fulfil it as well the anointing to flow, and the calling is a complete package. On your journey you will have to learn to flow in the anointing there is a price to pay. It is by faith that you will learn to will flow in the anointing that he will place upon, and in you. Now is the time you may be coming into the wilderness again, this is where you will learn to tap into the anointing not just learning to flow in it, but flow correctly.

1.   How to tap into the flow?
(a)   Learn to be quiet to hear that still small voice.
(b)   Make yourself available.
(c)   Step out on faith.
(d)   Prayer and Worship.
(e)   Love without love it accomplish you nothing.

Where ever it is that you should be flowing in it is in the wilderness that you will learn to flow on your way to the place call there I find myself flowing mostly in my writing, worship, and teaching. We must learn to flow in the anointing destroys the yoke of captivity. The anointing brings liberty to those that are bound Jesus tells us to take my yoke upon you for my yoke is easy, and my burden light if you will carry the yoke of Jesus, He promised you would learn of him and find rest unto your soul. The Lord's yoke is one of love, understanding, security and protection-an easy yoke, one that makes the burdens light.

There is a Process

Even when in transition, we should take the opportunity to proclaim the gospel we have this burden to see the lost save, especially in family member, even though some want to understand your change of life. The scriptures declare that you are a new creature in Christ Jesus old things are passed away and behold all things have become new. They still see you in the flesh and not the spirt because the process that you are going through. During you process you will have to read, pray, and be around mature believers, it is a sanctification process. You will have to stay focus and keep your eyes on Jesus it is easy to look at people in church system and get offended and throwed off you will have to grow up and get equipped, for the work of the ministry.

All members have a role to play or should I say fulfill in the process, and if you do not understand what you are going through you will quit. If God has helped you work through a problem, he can use you to help someone with the same problem he can use you. If he helps you overcome temptation and walk in holiness, he wants you to learn I in your process to help someone else to walk in holiness. If he helps you get through a difficult trail by leaning on him as strength and comfort, he wants to use you to help others to learn to trust him in similar trails. No one ever explain this to me this process so after the process to help someone through, he will use you even in the process. If you wait until you get it all together it will never happen no one have arrived yet, you are and will always be in process. Just keep your eyes on the sparrow, for Jesus is the author and finisher of your faith. In the process he makes intercession for us (you).

Romans 8:14-17,26

14. For as many as are led by the Spirit of God, they are the sons of God.
15. For you have not received the Spirit of bondage again to fear: but you have received the Spirit of Adoption, whereby we cry, Abba, Father.
16. The Spirit himself bear witness with our Spirit that we are the children of God.
17. And if children, then joint heirs; heirs of God, and join-heirs with Christ; if so be that we suffer with him, that we may be glorified together.
v. 26 Likewise the Spirit also help our infirmities: for we know not what we should pray for as we ought: but the Spirit himself make intercession for us with groaning which cannot be uttered.

Holy Spirit as Teacher

John 14:26

But the comforter, which is the Holy Ghost, whom the Father will send in my name, he shall teach you all things, and bring all things to you remember whatsoever; I have said unto you.

On your journey to your place called there you will get acquainted with your teacher, for you will become enrolled in the school of the Holy Spirit, He will become your best friend where you will ask all the question concerning the things of the kingdom. Your heart and your faith will be tested in this school get ready to learn who you are, and your purpose for being born and moving in the kingdom only God can revel this to you. Man can help confirm your purpose only God your creator knows your true purpose.

Nehemiah 9:20

You gave your good Spirit to instruct them, your manna you did not withhold from their mouth, and you gave them water do thirst.

Luke 12:12

For the Holy Spirit will teach you in the very hour what you should say.

These things have I written unto you concerning them that seduce you.

But the anointing which you have received of him abide in you and need not that any man should teach you: But as the same anointing teach you of all things, and is truth, and is no lie, and even as it hath taught you, you shall abide in him.

If we flow in Love the anointing will flow from God through you to whoever you are ministering to I believe we all should be lead, by the Holy Spirit who to witness to, who to minister healing and deliverance to it is the anointing that will destroy the yokes. Learning to tap into the anointing to flow like the rivers of living waters is a lesson from him. God is concern about our spiritual condition he do not want us to be spiritually dead. What has happened to the oil of the anointing of the Holy Spirit? The fire must stay lit to serve the God of fire it is the fire that of love, power, and self- control.

Spiritual Warfare

Spiritual Warfare is fight within and without, it is conflict with the flesh, the world, and the devil, it is war and we must learn how to win the battle in each one. The Lord have given us the victory over, and in each one. On your journey there will be obstacles, setbacks, oppositions, trails, etc. It is your responsibility to learn how to win in each one, each area we have the tools to win.

1. The flesh there is so much in scriptures to learn to apply to winning over the flesh there is a war going on in your flesh. I wish someone had taught mc onc on one, or just plan to me what this faith walk was all about, but thanks be to my Lord and Savior he is faithful.

But I say, walk in the Spirit, and do not fill the lust desires of the flesh: for these are opposed to each other, to prevent you from doing what you would. But if you are led by the Spirit you are not under the Law.

Galatians 5:13-15

This is a call to freedom you were called to freedom in him, one of the fruits of the Spirit is Love, so that means to walk in the Spirit you will learn to love even when it is your enemy but the good news is you want be walking alone Jesus will never leave you, nor forsake you in this battle. Our fight is not like the world it is kingdom principles built upon the solid rock. The flesh is weak, but the Spirit is willing our thoughts are not like his thoughts, and our ways are not as his ways, for his thoughts and ways are much higher than our ways. if we walk in the Spirit will we will not fulfill the lust of the flesh the Spirit will win every time.

By the Spirit we put to death the deeds of the flesh you will have to declare war on your flesh daily and kill it he is Holy Spirit.

Romans 12:2

Do not be conformed to this world, but be transformed by the renewing of your mind, that you may prove what is the good and acceptable and perfect will of God. You have the mind of Christ and have been made one with him, so this mean you can think the same way Jesus think it is all in the process.

You have his DNA his blood flows through you don't wait until you face temptation to try to walk in the Spirit do it before temptation come, or you will lose the battle in your flesh. This is the main key to victory being transformed by the renewing of your mind.

Since this is spiritual battle it must be fought with and in the spirit, not carnal in the flesh. Renewing the mind by reading the scriptures to apply practical and spiritual application the struggle is real, but why are so many believers losing, the struggle with their flesh? I would say it is all in the process of learning and training we are in the army of the Lord, whether we chose to or not, once you were transferred out of the kingdom of darkness into the kingdom of light you were recruited into the army of the Lord you in it to win!

Ephesians 6:12

Our struggle is not against flesh and blood, but against principalities, against power, against rulers of darkness of this world, against spiritual wickedness in high places.

2 Corinthians 10:3-6

For though we walk in the flesh, we do not war in the flesh, for the weapons of our warfare are not carnal, but mighty through God, for the pulling down of strongholds, pulling down every imagination that exalt itself against the knowledge of God, bringing down every thought to the obedience of the Christ.

On your journey to the place call there you will learn that when you witness to others that are in the world, you will be rejected and mocked, because of their unbelief and your lifestyle. He has overcome the world meaning we will learn to follow him to overcome we are in the world but not of the world. We are not part of the world value the scriptures declare believers are set apart meaning living Holy., righteous life, being a light that shine in the darkness. Having to deal with the thing in the world, the legally system, the city we live in, the state we live in the federal, courts etc. Following Christ is a price we must pay it is costly, and we must count the cost, even battling with the religious system. We must work in the world, it is your point of contact for the opportunity to witness for Christ even if it is just living a lifestyle of Holiness set- apart.

Matthew 28:19

Go you therefore, and make disciples of all nations, baptizing them in the name of the father, son, and Holy Ghost.

Who are we called to reach? You must figure that one out for you personally the Lord will reveal to you, your specific assignment is to reach people in your sphere of influence.

Spiritual Conflict with the Devil

Therefore; put on the whole armor of God, so that when the evil day comes, you may be able to stand your ground, and after you have done all you can just stand.

Stand firm with the belt of truth buckled around your waist, with the breastplate of righteousness in place.

And with your feet shod with the readiness that comes from the gospel of peace.

Take the shield of faith, with which you can extinguish all the flaming arrows of the evil one.

Take the helmet of salvation and the sword of the spirit which is the Word of God.

And pray in the Spirit on all occasions with all kinds of prayers and requests.

Be alert and always keep on praying for all the Lord's people.

Ephesians 6:10-18

The conflict with Satan is spiritual, and therefore no weapons can be employed against me putting on the spiritual armor will give you victory over the strategy of the enemy. Satan is the father of lies and deception it pays to know the truth, therefore the belt of truth is important to get dress first, you will need the truth all the way. Putting on the truth for your own sanctification, and deliverance you will need the truth to set you free.

Breastplate of righteousness with Jesus being your righteousness, you are the righteousness of God in Christ Jesus our righteousness is as dirty rags.

Gospel of Peace

In Spiritual Warfare the enemy places dangerous obstacles in the path of advancing soldiers the enemy sets traps as we go into different territory, he set obstacles in our path to deceive or mislead us. You are going to need your gospel shoes for stability.

Shield of Faith

The enemy comes against your faith sowing seed about your Lord Jesus who is the author and finisher or your faith. Without faith it is impossible to please him he who comes to him must believe he is a rewarder of them diligently seek him.

Helmet of Salvation

The Helmet is to protect you head, preserving your thinking have it transformed by the Word keeping a straight and sober mind focus on the Gospel of Peace. The helmet of salvation is protection you from false doctrine.

Sword of the Spirit

The offensive weapon in the armor of God speaks of Holiness and power of the Word of God.

Man shall not live by bread alone, but by every word that proceeds out of the mouth of God.

Matthew 4:4

Mystery of Spiritual Warfare

Your prayers cause collision in the heavens God commands his angels and send signs and wonders as part of the battle is to overcome evil with good. Our spiritual tools are to press forward on the battlefield:

1st Heaven where man lives under this heaven in the earth realm, we can see the sun, moon, and the stars under the first heaven.

2nd Heaven where the spiritual battle with demons and angels take place.

3rd Heaven where God the father, the Son, and the Holy Spirit.

Focus on the second heaven where warfare, of the unseen forces, unseen attack, over geographic area. We are called to pull down territory demonic stronghold in certain areas. If the demons don't have legal right to stay the prayers are address to God to change the hearts of the people.

Jeremiah 17:1

The battle belongs to the Lord when I look back on some of my battles that I went through as I apply the Word to that situation, I do not know what to do in that crisis. When it was over the Lord reminds me, he was teaching me how to win in that battle. Victory belongs to Jesus if we just follow his lead in amazement and awe I wanted to fight the canal way, but he taught me his way through pray, praise and worship. If we call on him he will show us great and mighty things we do not know of I love the Psalms of King David. He was hiding in the cave from King Saul, David had so much time on his hand he begin to write of his love and passion for the Lord, he was training David in the wilderness.

King Saul died sometimes God will hide you and who you are until it is time for you to come out of your wilderness on your way to the place call there you will be in training and preparation God will use your experience and pain to as you are coming out your battles will keep you on your knees. When I think about his goodness and all he done for me my soul cry Hallelujah!

In the mist of your battles he will give you the peace that surpasses all understanding, through it all you will learn to stand, for he will make your feet like Hinds feet to walk in high places.

Habakkuk 3:9

You must become rooted and grounded in the faith and contend for the faith that was once delivered to the saints, but God will test your faith remember you are in the school of the Holy Ghost the only way your faith will grow is to have your faith exercised, through trails, and tribulations.

Idolatry

Idolatry- Worship of idols, adoration, reverence, devotion.

On your way to your place God will deal with idols in your heart, that need to come down we all have idols that we have built up in our heart when in the world. If he won't deal with your idols you want be able to love him with all your heart, soul and strength he deserves your deepest and strongest affection. He does not just want lip service he wants your heart he wants it all. Your idols offend the Lord your God you will not want to offend him. How is covetousness idolatry? Idolatry starts in the heart, it starts with an act of loving something or someone too much or more than God who is the giver of life and all things. It could be a girlfriend, a car, wife, husband money, approval of others, a business, job those idols need to come down! You are still in the process, but don't let it take too long the idols have to come down the sooner the better you will forward.

The bottom line is when anything or anyone stands in the way of you and your creator the praise and honor that he alone deserves it is considered idol worship and not worship unto God.

Exodus 20:3-4

You shall have no other gods before me. You shall not make for yourself an idol in the form of anything in heaven above or on earth beneath or in the waters below.

Colossians 3:5-6

Put to death what is earthly in you, sexual immorality, impurity, evil desire and covetousness, which is idolatry on this account of there the wrath of God is coming.

God destroys idols: He is the great idol destroyer. Because even good things can become idols, so we are told not to be idol worshipers. Anyone or anything that comes before God is consider idols here is a truth people get upset when you zoom in on the dead god who can't save or set free, for some medicines are people gods. I can hear some of you say, Deborah where did you get that idea? It is truth it is a fact in modern day people depend more on medicines, doctors, and diagnosis more than the report of the Lord. The scripture declares by claiming to trust God and his truth so many are sick and living below their means. It is a stronghold from the enemy of the soul to keep us in bondage and depend upon drugs and some form. Therefore, everything in us must die to the flesh, because there is no good thing in our flesh. Fornication and impurity guilt and passion, evil desires and especially greed, which is the same as worshiping false gods. Therefore, the scriptures declare the wrath his anger of God will come upon us idols have to come down!

2 Kings 17:15

They rejected his decrees and covenant he had made with their fathers and the warnings he had given then they followed worthless idols and themselves became worthless. They imitate the nations around them although the lord had ordered them, "Do not do as they do, and they did the things the Lord had forbidden them to do.

We are called to carry our cross daily; the believer life is not peaches and creams, if this was so then Jesus would have given us the type of example of how we suffer and live the Godly life in Christ I can testify that when God must correct you it is not pretty at all. When chastised you will wish you had listened, but if he keep correcting you and you don't get it you will keep going around and around until you finally say Yes Lord! We are in the service of the Lord married to him it is a spiritual walk and way of life he calls us friends the prophets cried out concerning spiritual adultery and idols worshipers. God is a spirit no one want to have a personal relationship with God spoke through the prophets they were God mouth piece, his messengers. There were false prophets who prophesy false vision and imagination of the people heart so, God gave them the idols that were in their hearts.

Idolatry is a major one of the major themes in the bible over thirty pagan gods.
1. Dagan- the god of the Philistines he we worshiped as a fertility god.
2. Baal-the god of the rain and dew.

3. Ashtoreth-goddess of love and fertility.
4. Egyptian god Osiris the king of the living.
5. Malek-god of the Ammonites the passing

Through of fire.
6. Dianna of Ephesus-Greek temple.

Just to name a few idol gods that were worshiped their influence was great they forgot the true and living God that brought them out of Egypt. Now he says, he will be our God and we will be his people the tabernacle of God is with men. If God dwells in our heart guess where the idols are? The idols are in your heart in his temple he wants to tear them down! We don't know what is in our heart until God reveal it to us the heart is deceitfully wicked who can know it? I will go into more details on the sin of the idols that are in our hearts since God hate idolatry even in the old testament, he had prophets to speak on his behalf. What are some of the modern time idols that we worship now?

The Idol of Money

The love of money is the root of all evil, it did not say money is the root of all evil but when money controls us or overtake us it becomes evil working evil. The love of money one will steal from his own brother. Money can become the idol that control you I believe this is where the sin of covetousness come in when one what another inheritance. This is a matter of the heart where If I get the man, I will get the money it is an idol in the heart if he is married he just might leave his wife for another woman. For the love of money husband and wives puts their spouse into insurance just to get insurance money this is a matter of the heart anything desire more than God is an idol.

Idol of Success

One of the ways we see the idol of success in our life is when suffering or failure surprise us. When we something does not go the way, we think it ought to go. This one has been or should I say was an idol for me I was on a roller coaster on the road to neverland and set-backs some things no matter how hard I work at it no matter how many hours I put into it I never succeed in it this is real revelation with a wake- up call if you will listen to me you will be able to realize your idol in your heart. This was my downfall idol want to be successful in the things that God did not create me to be successful in. the idol of success is a disappointing road you may be saying, Deborah it feels right and I say to you yes with all the money that you are making, you probably are going to be doing something to promote the kingdom of God. When plans are devasted we become devastated we live in a time when people think that their success will keep them safe from the troubles of life. Why did God keep raining on my parade? Because of the idol of success that was in my heart the only thing that did not play out in this idol of success is I did not step on anyone to get to the top, I never played the game of power play.

Naaman was a champion very successful he was highly favored he was a might man of valor he conquers every nations and army he comes up against he is respected, but is greatly respected but he had a problem, he has a skin disease all his success, wealth, achievement, and power could not cure his disease. With that in mind there is no amount of success that can keep bad things from happening to us. Remember on your way to the place call there don't forget to check your heart on a regular daily basis keep repentance before you God hates idols.

Idol of Marriage

A precious gift of God, or a false god of personal security? When does marriage becomes an idol? When anxiety and fear of losing a man or woman that God have lend to you. When you a wife is not able to function in the ministry that God called her to do, and when I speak of ministry it is not just standing behind a pulpit, for ministry is service unto the Lord. Ministry is in the home and could be in the church, or in the world God should be our peace and security, our hope, and joy.

Matthew 10:37

Whosoever loves father, mother more than me is not worthy of me, and whoever loves son or daughter more than me is not worthy of me."
Do you talk about your husband, or wife more than you talk about Jesus? Do you mention the Lord; unless it is about him blessing you? Do you boast about a man or woman who can become ill at the drop of a hat just, because they are human, they can fall? Do you bow down to a man or woman, because you see them as a god? Well, this is call an idol marriage I am not saying you are not to love and not respect your spouse that is not what I am trying to bring out. The truth of the matter   you are not to put them before God even your children. God hates idols worshiper even if you put self on high. The truth will set us all free. Marriage is a metaphor created by God to represent future union of God to his pure church. Marriage is temporary the body of Christ is eternal marriage is not the goal, but marriage is of the law. Marriage help us get consecrate for the master use my point is that God consecrate us through marriage being married to one man or woman help us to become Holy the goal is to be transform into the image

of Christ.

Ephesians 5:22-23

"Wives submit yourselves to your own husbands as unto the Lord. For the husband is head of the wife, even as Christ is head of the church: and he is the savior of the body. Therefore, the church is subject unto Christ so let the wives be subject to their own husband in everything. Husband love your wives even as Christ also love the church and gave himself for it; that he may sanctify and cleanse it with the washing of the water of the word that he may present to him a glorious church not having spot, or wrinkle, or any such thing, but is shall be holy without blemish.

Mark 12:25

For when they rise for the dead, they neither marry nor given in marriage, but are like angels in heaven.

The church places a lot of emphasis on marriage, it is not like we will marry in the resurrection, which is eternal. I know a many of you want to agree with me but has become a deception in the body, because people are marring for the wrong reason when we are to not be like the world but set apart. We are to be kingdom builders it is not all about a marriage, it is about winning soul to the kingdom. The world comes in and get the pastors to marry them at the expense of the kingdom. When do marriage becomes an idol? When people don't recognize that marriage is a metaphor. I am not against marriage I am married Jesus is the best thing that ever happen to me I just want to reveal how the enemy have taken another precious gift of God and turn it into a deception.

1 Corinthians 7:28

"But those who marry will face many troubles in this life, and I want to spare you this. I would like you to be free from concern. An unmarried man is concerned about the Lord's affairs how he can please the Lord. But a married man is concerned about affairs of this world how he can pleas his wife that's when it becomes Idolatry God hates idolatry."

Idol of Approval

Being a people pleaser is the idols in today society approval isn't a bad thing, but when we crave approval it becomes an idol. This struggle is real for the majority or society, working at being people pleaser that's' hard work. I just want to do and be who I am in Christ I don't want to be like no one else only be Deborah I heard a minister say, "Before you can ever be yourself, you have to actually like you like yourself the way out of hating yourself isn't being like someone else. The idol of approval is so, serious that people want you to be like them, get comfortable with your own skin, be a God pleaser and not a people pleaser. Your identity will be found in Jesus and only Jesus I meet people all the time who say they know who they are, but their stagnation says something different. Ever heard the saying action speaks louder than words? Show me your action, and I will believe your words. In Christ we don't need an image for our identity nor can anyone take it away. Our fake for approval won't go away.

On your way to the place call there you will need the freedom from others' approval ask yourself who approval do you seek the most? Do you have a hard time going a day without going around people you need approval from? Do you have a hard time accepting God's approval? This is all the approval that you need. Do you compare yourself to others? Does the success of others intimidate you making you feel inadequate? Do you need to do good deeds to be seen? Do you need the Love and attention of others to get approval can pull a few of these out for myself, but for long time I need the approval of others, but if I need their approval I will become like Saul people pleaser Idol of approval, What?

Ephesians 1:5-6

To the praise of the glory of his grace. Where he hath made us accepted in the beloved.

Matthew 3:17

And behold, a voice out of heavens said, this is my beloved son, in whom I am well pleased.

How do we overcome idol? We overcome by seeing, and following the Christ, yes! it is time to focus and focus on him, so keep your eyes on the sparrow. Jesus id the way, the truth, and the life on your way to the place call there. I believe the key is to humble yourself under the mighty hand of God and he will exalt you in due season. If we or going to please God, we cannot search for the approval of others he is the creator of all things he knows the number of hairs in your head. I don't know about you, but I want to please him, and going down to straight and narrow path there will be many opposition that will come against you just because you serve Jesus.

Matthew 10:25

"Woe unto you when everyone speaks well of you, for their fathers treated the false prophets the same way." There is no escape with enemies, if they called Jesus the master Beelzebub, how much more will they call those in their household?

Which means if Jesus was criticized, how much more you who follow Jesus will be criticized, because the world is full of critic. "Woe to you on your way to the place call there when people speak well of you and you get off track". You want to know how to overcome, and respond to those who revolt against you? One of the beatitude is hard to master, but remember you are a work in process. Love your enemies, do good to those who despise you or despitefully use you. It is a hard pill to swallow especially when we have been taught about getting revenge in the world, because we also have enemies in our own household who despise Jesus. He has overcome the world to give us victory in him this journey is full of obstacles and pitfalls when moving from one level in him to another level in him make sure you get your orders from the chief in command Jesus. The places you will go some will be unfamiliar, but you will have to trust him in all your ways he will direct you path it is all a testing of your faith and love for him.

Trails come and Go

The Holy Spirit impressed upon me the tree in scripture it talks about the trees as peoples it is a metaphor like fish. I ask Lord why trees it is because when planting trees, they are planting in soil starts out as seeds trees then takes roots. Within the family tree there are roots in other word generation to generation. I became so interested in the symbols of trees I begin to do study on the family tree where the roots of the tree begin with unforgiveness being the seed of bitterness, this tree is the root of bitterness an unhealthy tree. Because of our genes in the family tree from one generation to another generation the family tree become unhealthy trees. The root starts with anger and passed down from one generation to another as life bring in the bad we even get anger with God this is where one blame God for not preventing a tragedy or illness that destroyed a life or marriage. Now because people worship and idolize marriage, and there; health will fail they blame God or should I say we blame God I have done it too. We make lots of wrong decisions my life was full of wrong decisions after decisions no good judgement on anything everything I did fail it would start off good, but the end always ended bad. Who did I blame? God of course he didn't love me, he did protect me, he didn't warn me, he didn't exist. You not real God! If you were real you would have helped me out of this mess God gives warning signs and what we do? We ignore them the signs. I was so simply and blind to the wiles of the devil in our family growing up the enemy manifest himself very heavily in our family.

Anger towards God: Seed planted unforgiveness=bitterness

    1.   Hatred

2. Rage
3. Revenge
4. Resentment

Murder Memory recall of hurts - Retaliation
1. Family feuds-Accusation
2. Alcoholism-Fighting
3. Drug Addiction-Gluttony
4. Occultism-Blindness
5. Anger-Sugar Diabetes
6. Nicotine- Arthritis
7. Witchcraft-Heart Problems
8. Racial Hatred-Anorexia
9. Rage-Cancer

There you have it the tree of bitterness with the seed being unforgiveness.

"Beloved think it not strange concerning the fiery trail which is to try you, as though some strange thing happened unto you. That the trail of your faith being much more precious than gold that perish, though it be tried with fire might be found unto praise and honor and glory at the appearing of Christ.

1 Peter 4:12-17

The Lord sometimes lets things happen that we don't understand to test us and try us he places us in the refiners' fire of trails and test us to bring us to boil, so all the scum and dross come to the surface to purge us out. The fire is to bring out the meanness and bitterness in us he can also put us on the potters' wheel, to make, shape, and mold us to become who he called you to be. Suffering can either make you are break you, become bitter or sweet, it should bring out the bring you, not the worst which is called bitterness.

Bitter Sweet Bitterness often comes out of abuse, cruelty, rejection, and disappointment.

Isaiah 53:2-5

For he shall grow up before him as a tender plant, and as a root out of a dry ground: he hath no form more comeliness; and when we shall see him, there is not beauty that we should desire him. He is despised and rejected of men; a mon of sorrow and acquainted with grief; and we hid as it were our faces form him; he was despised, and we esteemed him not. He hath borne our griefs and carried our sorrow: Yet we did esteem him stricken, smitten of god, and afflicted. But he was wounded for our transgression, he was bruised for our iniquities: the chastisement of our peace was upon him; and by his stripes we are healed.

Isaiah 53:7

He was oppressed, and he was afflicted, yet he opened not his mouth: he is brought as a lamb to the slaughter, and as a sheep before her shearers is dumb so he opened not his mouth.

Luke 23:34

"then said Jesus, father, forgive them; for they no not what they do. And they parted his raiment and cast lots."

The Tree of Rejection

This tree has to do with paranoia, isolation, depress, suicide, mental illness, schizophrenia the tree bears the fruit of bitter roots, with the inability to receive love; it makes us feel unworthy. It also; bear the fruit of inability to love others, the inability to trust others, bear the fruit of insecurities that come with betrayal or criticism. Withdrawal is another fruit feeling vulnerable in the presence of others, another is suspicion the suspicious that one might be rejected. Shyness and fear of failure, fear of man, fear of rejection, and self-rejection. But if you just strip the leaves off the branches, they'll return, and if we cut off a branch they will return. If you chop down the whole tree you not getting to the root of the problem. If you get to the root of the matter you can weed it out once and, for all this tree is different from the tree of bitterness in the sense this tree is rooted in false beliefs:

Fear of Rejection   Perceived Rejection

- Perfection-Control   * Bitterness-offence
- Anger-aggression * Isolation-Loneliness
- People-Pleaser   * Jealousy-competition
- Rejection of Others   * Self- Rejection
- Suspicious-Mistrusting * insecurities
- Comparison   * Self- Pity
- Fear of Failure   * Poor self -image
- Anxiety-Worry   * Depression

There is so much in this chapter I would like to stay here, but I must move on and encourage you to do a study on this deeply stronghold called root of bitterness and unforgiveness it has helped me just writing about it. I believe we all have some deliverance to deal with and things we need to overcome I never realized that so many people were in so much pain with deep scars. We are the bitter generation in denial need deliverance and healing form our past and childhood struggles. We are not ready for the family, houses, cars, marriage; job promotion, more money, we are in preparation the process stage being processed out. On your way to the place call there you will encounter what you call soul searching, this is where they will help you find your roots. He will bring you through, and out of the religious belief systematic where your belief will change from going through a form of godliness with not power and authority of the Word.

You will have opposition in this place too especially from the religious just as Jesus did people do not want to leave their comfort zone they are comfortable where they are being stagnated. It is a routine of one in their daily walk Jesus reveal, exposed, manifest, the supernatural power of God he was the great example. You will need a transitional shift a major change in your life to another way of doing things, and a new way of doing things being stuck in a routine is too easy. How will you find your place in the body if you don't step out on faith out of your comfort zone.

Habakkuk 2:4

The just shall live walk by faith.

Galatians 3:11

But that no man is justified by law I the sight of God, it is evident: for the just shall live by faith.

Applying the Application

Learning to apply the Word to your circumstance, because the Word is alive, it is quick and powerful than two edge Sword putting into practice what we learn and mediate on. You will want to read it daily, memorize it, apply it to your life. He is the living Word he is alive God not dead he is alive. Then let us hide his Word in us that we may not sin against him obeying his commandments. Studying and, memorizing, and meditating on what you have read making it possible to apply the scriptures. You will to allow the Word to "take root" in your heart this is an important application to learn on your way to your place.

James 1:21-22

Wherefore lay aside filthiness and superficial of naughtiness, and receive the engrafted Word, which can save your souls.

22. But be doers of the word, and not hearers only, keep, maintain this word to apply it to your life situations and circumstances in your life.

Just remember the believer life is not just about getting to heaven, it is also the present life, and about growing more in the likeness of Jesus Christ You will learn to love reading and studying the scripture as the Spirit will sanctify you, because he dwells in you.

John 17:17

Sanctify them in the truth; your word is truth.

The sanctification process there is the building of character, being " set apart as pure" and purified for a vessel of honor this prayer of sanctification Jesus for the ones the father gave, before the foundation of the world, means that every law, stature, illustration, example, and principle is good for us that is sanctified and set apart helping us have a better life now by building godly character in us.

A Battle Cry

It is a time for weeping and the Spirit of God will weep and groan through you if you answer the call to intercessory prayer. When I begin to read the book of Lamentation, just reading it I would begin to weep, and I could not control it, so I ask another dreamer in the group. What is this? She explained to me the Holy Spirit is weeping through you and none of my tears will go unnoticed by god. Wow! Weeping I was reminded of the Prophet Jeremiah a weeping prophet, here is the curiosity of the weeping I was always wondering why did he weep? But he called for the wailing, and weeping women of his day as born- again believers we need to allow the Holy Spirit to cry, to pray through us when the unction comes upon us he will help you pray through, even why you are weeping.

Romans 26:27

The Spirit also helps in our weaknesses for we do not know what we should pray for as for as we ought, but the spirit himself makes intercession for us with groaning which cannot be uttered. Now he who searches the hearts knows what the mind of the spirit is, because he makes intercession for the saints according to the will of God.

As you allow the weeping unction of the Holy Spirit to cry out through us, we will be praying for the things for which the Spirit within us is weeping, in the way the Lord wants it prayed about, and in the will of the Lord for the outcome.

Romans 8:28

And then we know that all things work together for the good to those who love God, to those who are called according to his purpose.

Let the Spirit of the Lord lead you in the battle cry let him direct you to pray according to his will pray it through." Until you have a release in your spirit or peace in your spirit. Weeping brings great harvest and is one of the expressions of the Holy Spirit in intercession whenever the Spirit weeps in us, we are bearing seeds of deliverance, salvation and breakthrough. The weeping is a weeping that comes either in silences or loud as though in great distress being in tune with the Spirit of God will keep you in the right direction, this weeping of prayer never was taught to me coming up in church, but when the weeping begins with me I had to search deeper for what was going on. Your tears cause God to act, and the enemy to react weeping for God to turn the hearts of the nations and cities is spiritual warfare, and intercessory prayer.

Let the will of God be done in the battle, not your will, but his will that is what Jesus prayed Jesus is the great role model for prayer. But he is our high priest who is continually praying for the believer go from faith to faith. Jesus is the author and finisher of your faith praise, worship, prayer, intercession, in a real battle with a real enemy, but the out simple things God use to confound the wise, tears, weeping, travailing, groaning, wailing.

The heart is deceitful above all things, and desperately wicked: who can know it?

I the Lord search the heart, I try the reins, even to give every man according to his ways, and according to the fruits of his doing.

Jeremiah 17:7

The fruit of his doing. What? Good fruit, bad fruit, the fruit of his doing, this tree thing is big in the kingdom of God symbolic to people growing or producing fruits. It is our hearts that determine what happens through prayer I never saw this, the fruits of your doing. God need us to tear down the high places that are in our heart because he is a God of the heart prepare for the battle god wants your tears to help bring a harvest into the nations.

Where is your Testimony?

Where is your testimony? You will need to have a testimony to help someone else on this journey to you place he call you out of darkness into his marvelous light. You may not be proud of your past, but your testimony will help someone else. On this journey I have met people who are hurting need to hear a true testimony to help someone else you must be free. If you have a story to tell make sure you give it and make sure you are free from the stronghold in your life if you don't get free from your stronghold the enemy will have a legal right to stop you hold you in bondage, accused you of lying. Where is your testimony?

Revelation 12: 11

They overcome by the blood of the Lamb, and word of their testimony; and they love not their life unto death.

Satan's house remains in the heavens, coming before the Throne of God day and night, accusing the saints of all their wrongs.

Revelation 12:10

Then I heard a loud voice in heaven say:

Now have come salvation and the power and the kingdom of our God, and authority of his Christ. For the accuser of our brothers, who accuses them before our God day and night, has been cast down.

Our heavenly father is also the judge, Satan comes as a prosecutor accusing us day, and night so you will need to overcome him by the word of your testimony in the courts of heaven. We are being prepared in our process to judge the world, and the angels therefore some of us go through so much with court system he wants us to learn from our experience. Where is your testimony? I would say it is in the Blood of the Lamb because the enemy can't prevail against the perfect righteousness of the blood of the Lamb. If he can bring us out from under the cleansing blood he can win and prevail.

This means war I plea, I plea, the blood tells him you are under the blood, your testimony is in the blood, and your life is under the blood for you were saved by his blood look at the cross where he shed his blood and delivered you from the power of darkness. If any man be in Christ he is a new creature old thing are passed away, behold all things have become new.

Make a joyful noise unto the Lord, all ye lands
2.   Serve the Lord with gladness; come before his presence with singing
3.   Know ye that the Lord is God: it is he that hath made us and not we ourselves; we are his people, and the sheep of his pasture.
4.   Enter his gates with thanksgiving, and into his courts with praise; be thankful unto him and bless his name.
5.   For the Lord is good; his mercy is everlasting; and his truth endure to all generations.

The Blood of Jesus will never lose its' power his blood is a once saving grace no more animals he is the precious Lamb of God. The Blood of Jesus cleanse us from all unrighteousness.

" Therefore brethren, having boldness to enter the Holiest by the blood of Jesus, by a new and living way which He consecrated for us, through the veil that is His flesh, and having a High Priest over the house of God , let us draw near with a true heart in full assurance of faith, having our hearts sprinkled from evil conscience and our bodies washed with pure water.

Hebrew 10:19-

Spiritual Midwife- Intercessory Prayer

On your Journey to your place you will begin find that place in him where you will help other born- again believer birth out their purpose in the kingdom. You will find that through your time alone with God, he will endow, equip you with power from on high to help others in deliverance, and fill them with his Spirit. Come into this place of spiritual midwife – intercessory prayer will amaze you, because as you step out on faith into this realm of no return, your faith will increase in his supernatural power.

Exodus 1:15-21

The King of Egypt said, to the Hebrew Midwives their names were Shiphrah and Puah, 16 When you are helping the Hebrew women during childbirth on the delivery stool, if you see that the baby is a boy, kill him; but if it is a girl, let her live. 17. The midwives, however, feared God and did not do what the king of Egypt had told them to do; they let the boys live. 18. Then the king of Egypt summoned the midwives and asked them Why have you done this?" 19. The midwives answered Pharaoh, Hebrew women are not like Egyptian women; they are vigorous and give birth before midwives arrive. 20. God was kind to the midwives and the people increased and became even more numerous. 21. And because the midwives feared God, he gave them families of their own."

I am in a state of awe how the Lord give his people the blood wash people to do the work of the ministry. If you are in the kingdom a believer, we are to help in the deliverance to bring forth babies through intercessory prayer, weeping, wailing, travailing and groaning, the Lord is calling you to a deeper walk in him.

My Dream of giving Birth

In the year of 2013, the Lord begin to deal with me heavy in dreams and visions I was dreaming day and night. I began to seek the Lord more to understand of my dream most of my dreams was always dreaming about my car past car present car. When I had the dream concerning the blood of Jesus, as I wrote in my first book the mystery of the kingdom I had no clue to these meanings. I did not know that my journey to my place call there was a journey to finding out my true ministry concerning dreams, visions, and revelations. In October 2013 the Lord begin to visit me often in dreams I know it was his presence that was there upon my awakening. There was always peace I the room after I awake from my sleep it was the peace that surpassed all understanding. In that year I had dream I was surrounding by these people in what seem like a hospital room and bed these people were helping me push the baby out, after it was over, I set my eyes upon a beautiful baby boy wrapped in a light blue blanket. My brother Milford was the baby there were other family members too. I got up from the bed went into the bathroom to wash my hands and face. I did not know I was pregnant in the Spirit I was carry a spiritual baby for him. Upon awaken I asked, "What was that dream about? but I was feeling so refresh and spiritually high I did begin a search about dreams, and vision I was amazed at what I found this is how I begin my journey on dreams, visions, and revelations. I join a group dream team for the interpretations of dreams on, Facebook I was so amazed at these people interpreting dreams and visions. I post my dreams I was so excited about this new profound mystery that I did not know. I have been on that journey since October 25, 2013. I seek the Lord on that beautiful baby that he births out of me. I receive the meaning of the colors, and signs. Therefore, to help someone else you must have experience in you calling, ministry, business a midwife must know the principles of being a midwife.

I had given birth to a dream, vision, and a purpose for my life for which the Lord had called me if one give birth in the natural it will have to be nourished and grow. In those days I was really into the posture of laying on my face before God in prayer. I used to go to this place called, the secret places a little chapel in a little town call Mesquite open twenty-four hour; seven days a week I was weeping before the Lord almost every day. Weeping brings forth deliverance, salvation, and breakthrough. My spiritual baby is four years old this year 2018. I have care for him, nourished him with my Prayers, the Word, Praise and Worship. Obeying the instruction of the Lord so my spiritual baby could grow into a healthy ministry, purpose, for the Lord to get the glory you never know where the Lord will take you on this journey to your place call there. You will need a healthy delivery and no problems to occur in the process of bring forth the lord vision and purpose for your life. Get ready for this exciting journey if you love adventure you will love your journey with him. Why did I have this experience? My answer is so I could help someone else in the body of believers in Christ. Do you believe the Lord want you to be ignorant about the spiritual things of God? Do you believe the Lord save you to sit still in the church and not grow spiritually? However, he wants you to get it just follow his lead and obey his voice he will never leave you, forsake you if you must birth out books like I did start keeping journals. If a magazine, poetry, teaching, preaching, music; just follow Jesus as his sheep get it done before, he returns most of your ministry and calling will come through your experience in life and in the church life, so get ready to take in every lesson the Lord will teach you even through others. Your experience might even come through your mate, or children.

Midwife -noun mid- a person or thing who aids in producing something new.

You will have to aid one way or another there is no way you should be sitting on the sideline doing nothing even spiritual midwives are an important part of the body of Christ. The way one find his or her purpose or calling is through your prayer that is personal time with God intercession is how you will know the true from the lukewarm, you will be giving birth through your service to God the midwife is the hand in the body which is the gift of service and helps in other words the spiritual midwives are the hands God use for his service. Midwives work mostly behind the scene to bring forth spiritual birthing they are needed to hold people hands and remind us to breathe. Those who will help give birth to something new and be transformed through faith midwives understand the process of giving birth.

1 Corinthians 12:27-28

Now you are the body of Christ and, members.

And God have set some in the Church, first apostles, second prophets, third teachers, after that miracles, then gifts of healing, helps, governments, diversities of tongues.

Oholiab was gifted by God as a helper to Bezalel, the craftsman with the gift of service. God gifted him to beautify the tabernacle. I it had not been for the gifted servants and helpers who constructed it there would have been no tabernacle.

Exodus 31:1-6

The Lord also spoke to Moses: Look I have appointed by name Bezalel son of Uri son Hurl of the tribe of Judah. I have filled him with God's Spirit with wisdom, understanding, and ability in every craft to design artistic works in gold, silver, and bronze, to cut gemstones for mounting and to carve wood for work in every craft. I have also selected Oholiab son of Hismaic of the tribe of Dan to be with him.

I believe if you find your place in the kingdom on your journey to you place it will make you whole but there are those who will oppose you and think they are doing God a service, which is out of his service. The scriptures tell us to let every man, work out his own soul salvation with fear and trembling. Don't take your eyes of the prize, things are working together for your good. If you suffer with him, you will reign with him. This is what was birth out of me writing books for the kingdom of God becoming an author , learning to publish my own work after making some errors going through some people who was not for me no one properly taught me to write learning how to write and publish was and is a process for me ,but he let me know he birth it out of me so I have to take care and protect of what he gave me. I have not yet arrived no one have I am happy about me accomplish but the glory belongs to God the creator of all things. I understand natural and spiritual midwives to help someone you must have an experience or encounter with the spirit world as well as the natural. I am in a place of wholeness I love what I do I am a peace with God and myself yes, the enemy still try to stop me that's his job no more depressed thoughts, not more feeling of loneliness I know my purpose I know my calling I am a living testimony. In writing these books I pray that someone get set free to his or her destiny I pray that some of you get delivered and set free from your strongholds I pray that someone find and have a real personal encounter with Jesus Christ son of the living God. I am in Christ Jesus pressing toward the mark of the high calling in Christ Jesus. I am redeemed, I am healed, I am a new creature, I am made complete in him, I am washed by the blood, I am free to flow in the anointing, I am the righteousness of god in Christ. I am seated in high places in Christ I am a living epistle.

On your way to your place call there he will make your feet like hinds' feet to walk in high places he has brought me a mighty long way, and when I look back over my life from where I use to be as to where I am now. How can I set and not give him the praise and glory that truly belongs to him and him alone? I should have been gone long ago, but he allowed me more chance than I can count he allow me to stick around until I come to my -self, because of his mercy and grace and the prayers of my grand sister Ca 'miller Jones. I am an overcomer a survival. Thank you, Lord Jesus for saving me and dying on the cross so I am live the life you purpose for me go ahead find your purpose.

An Overview of the Body of Christ

In the body of Christ, we have the eyes of those who see in the spirit realm the eyes of the Lord some can see angels, demons, they have the gift of discerning of spirits we all can discern others that are not in the spirit who are carnal minded. To see or perceive by the eye is to see, to have knowledge of, observe, discern, or understand. Spiritual sight is not the use of the natural or physical eye. It will take the oil of the lamp of the light, and the fire of God to keep your light shining, so the eyes in the body will not go dim or go out. To be spiritually blind is to be deceived and one think they can see. The devil is a master on big deception he deceives eve in the garden.

Revelation 3: 17:19

You say I am rich I have acquired wealth and do not need a thing. But you so not realize that you are wretched, pitiful, poor, blind, and naked. I counsel you to buy from me gold refined in the fire, so you can become rich; and white cloths to wear, so you can cover your shameful nakedness; buy salve to put on your eyes, so you can see. Those whom I love I rebuke and discipline. Be honest and repent!

Another Dream

In this Dream I was taken in the Spirit by way of car the dream went like this: I was driving in this car I had two or r three other passengers with me. I find myself driving pulling up in front of a Church as I let these people out in front of the church I decide I would go park the car and then join them in church. When I begin to back up the car too off in the air going backwards here I am in a car flying backwards in the air. The people that got out of the car start waving at me say as though they were saying bye thank you for the ride. As I was flying backwards I saw the face of Jesus like a movie screen then I looked down I saw this orange-red big sea like it look like people were in there waving like they like they were trying to get out. I ask the Lord, what is this is see? He said, the lake of fire for a moment I thought I was going I said; oh! no I flew right over in the car then I saw the Eagle, and the Lion. Wow! That was close. The car kept going flying backwards finally I landed on this Island where I saw just a man and a monkey, then the dream ended.

Seeing in the spirit comes in more than one form there are those who have prophetic dreams and visions, there are those who can see in the spirit when awake giving prophecy.

The point I am trying to make is that none of us in the body of Christ operate the same in the gift of prophecy this is surely a point the Holy Spirit want me to make here. God has placed in the body his gifts they are not our gifts all have their own personalities this is not about competing that is how the world and their system operate through competition. It is time for the people of God to find their rightful place in the kingdom we are helpers one to another. If you want to see miracles happen get one accord, unity in oneness.

The Ears in the Body

Now we come to the ears in the body of Christ looking at the tabernacle in the wilderness is a shadow- type for the new testament believers from the gates to the outer court to the Holy place to the Holy of Holies. Other names are: Ark of the covenant and Mercy Seat. Now that the veil was torn from top to bottom we are the temple where God dwells. Coming into his presence with thanksgiving and praise not only do we talk, but we learn to listen this is what the ears do in the body, but we can all listen we learn to listen for it is an art. When we give thanks and praise to our God not only do we talk to him we are to wait on him to speak this is what the ears do in the body let him that has ears hear what the spirit is saying to the church. We need to posture ourselves to hear. It becomes a two- way conversation between you and God. when you pray say:

Our Father, who art in Heaven

Hallowed be thy name,
Thy kingdom come Thy will be done on earth as it is in heaven give us this day our daily bread and forgive us our trespasses against us and lead us not into temptation but deliver us from evil for thine is the kingdom, and the power, and the glory, forever and ever. Amen
Prayer is the key to all your avenues on your destiny to your place call there whatever the Lord have called you are who every you are in him prayer is the key that unlocks your doors to your identity, Men are to always pray, and not faint. Always does not mean we have to neglect the ordinary duties of life; what it means is that the soul that has come into intimate contract with God in the silence of the prayer chamber is never out of touch with the father of light.

Hinderance to prayer:
    1.   Unconfessed sin in the heart of the one who is praying and living according to the flesh our ability to communicate with God and be led by the

Spirit the number one hinderance is unconfessed sin in our life.

2. Unforgiveness – A root of bitterness comes from the seed of unforgiveness that springs up in our heart it chokes our prayers, so they go un answered.

3. Selfishness- asking God for what we want, not his will for our life or a situation is a wrong motive, and that hinders our prayers we need to ask him thy will be done.

4. Unbelief and doubt-doubting his character, purpose, and his promises is rejecting God and his Word, for rejection comes under another tree.

5. Sowing Discord- sowing discord seeds, lying. Backbiting, jealousy, envy, strife, malice, covetousness, and such like. What so ever a man sows that shall he reap.

These are some of the hinderance to our prayers the scriptures say, God will not hear us, so prayer is the key to all your avenues to your destination, always di a heart check at every level. Prayer is the key to all if you stay prayed up, and if you stumble you will not fall. It is very safe and important to keep a pray life, because when the enemy comes in lie a flood the Spirit of the Lord will raise up a standard against him.

Sing in my dream

LORD WE ADORE AND WORSHIP YOUR HOLY NAME, HOLY NAME. HOLY NAME, LORD WE WORSHIP AND ADORE YOUR HOLY NAME, HOLY NAME, HOLY NAME, LORD WE WORSHIP AND ADORE YOUR HOLY NAME, HOLY NAME, HOLY NAME.

I Dream I was walking, and all the sudden wolves many wolves, packs of wolves come toward me it was so many wolves. My daughter Crystal and I was walking together for those who know she is always with me. We were walking these wolves were observing us they begin coming toward us. I picked her up threw her around my neck and begin to sing as I was singing I was walking the wolves begin to disappear one by one. I kept walking and singing looking toward the sky I saw a man figure in the clouds looked like fire. I kept staring it looked like Jesus in the cloud disappeared I kept walking, and singing I saw people were running and were afraid I then saw Jesus then I woke up feeling refresh and light.

New Grounds

You will gain new grounds and the enemy will try to make you lose and give up your territory, but after you gain your ground you must maintain your ground. The plan God have for you is to succeed in the kingdom the plan the enemy have for you is to be deceived, so he has no new tricks they are old the good news is we must learn his strategy as come with false teachers and doctrines the wolves in sheep clothing. His plan is to lead you astray off the path that you are on for the Lord talking from experience I have been I church and out of church most of my life. If you learn the real, then you won't have to worry about being deceive you will learn what is fake. In my faith walk I was introduced to the real then when the fake came I sense something was not right. Now I live to right about it I do not expect everyone to agree with my writing because there are many carnal minded flesh so call Christians.

Beware of false prophets, who come to you in sheep's clothing but inside are ravenous wolves.

Matthew 7:15

Dreaming of wolves looking like dogs.

Wailing Women

In this group that we started call wailing women at the well a pray group for praying women crying out to the Lord waking -up early every morning to pray. Going your way, you may meet some sincere praying women it is not a bad thing, but make sure you are praying to the same God. Every morning six o'clock a.m. we were on the phone line praying this went on about a good two years there were only two left, but we carried on in prayer. Sister Anita Smith, and me Debora faithfully crying out to him calling ourselves wailing women. My dear sister Anita Smith came up with the wailing women at the well in 2010. God bless you my sister I met you the same year and we bonded in the Spirit. This have been a blessing in our life to cry our interceding on the behalf of others on our journey we met others, but they did not stay but we were faithful to the cause Meeting others will help you sharpen your skills, gifts, talent and directions, at the same time you will me those that are not going your way. All in all, it is a journey where you must make tough decision to trust in the Lord and he will direct thy path.
Jesus said, out of your belly shall flow rivers of living waters.
Therefore, when Jesus come to the well there was a woman there at the well drawing water from the well. Jesus asked, her for a drink of water.
And he must needs go through Samaria, which is called Chary, near to parcel of ground that Jacob gave to his son Joseph.
Now Jacobs' well was there Jesus therefore, being wearied with his journey, sat there on the well: and it was about the six hours.

There came a woman of Samaria to draw water: Jesus said unto her, give me to drink.

For his disciples were gone away unto the city to buy meat.

Then said, the woman of Samaria unto him, how is it that you a Jew, ask drink of me, which am a woman of Samaria? For the Jews had no dealing with the Samaritans.

Jesus answered and said unto her, if you knew the gift of God, and who it is that said to you, give me to drink; you would have asked him, and he would have given you living water.

Jesus conversation with this Samaritan woman who had to get water from a well which was Jacob's well this well was located about half mile from the city of Sychar in Samaria. As I read story, this woman was an outcast.

Making a Vow

What about the vow Hannah made to God? Hannah not only prayed for a son she made a promise to God! O Lord Almighty, if you will look down upon my sorrows and answer my prayer and give me a son, then I will give him back to you. After a year a weaning Hannah fulfilled her vow by giving Samuel to Elis' care. Hannah learned how to hold onto Gods' provision and no mans' provision for his provision is everlasting. I read this story about Hannah, she was an ordinary woman with an extraordinary character one of integrity. She did not go back to her promise to God. This noble principle is a good character, listen we are given us in prayer. She became impregnate with a man child through prayer. I realize there are biblical principles, and they were given for our example. It is a shadow type of the footsteps of Jesus. Can you see this? God gave his only begotten son away to be raised from the dead for our sin.

Jeremiah 25:36

A voice of the cry of the shepherds and a howling of the principal of the flock, shall be heard: for the Lord hath spoiled their pastures.

The Seed is planted in prayer

Those that travel alone the way and those that come to church on Sunday and the devil takes the seed out of their hearing, so they can't believe if you keep the word you will believe. If the devil steal. the seed then I can't believe. You need a seed in your heart to believe. Those upon the rock receive the seed with joy but, have no roots in time of trail and temptation the cares of this world. It is the attack of the enemy on the seed the enemy is after the seed if there is no root the seed won't grow. When Hannah prayed and prayed the seed was planted through prayer for her seed to continue to grow, she had to preserve in prayer water her seed. I imagine she travail in prayer, because Eli the priest thought she was drunk. She prayed so much with continual prayer; until she was drunk in the Spirit. Even though this is a practical application it is a spiritual application for the new birth church. I started off on my journey in prayer wanting to know him in ways I had not known him before I had gotten a glimpse of the supernatural God in the bible I knew it was more to what I had experience in church.

What is the Purpose of the church?

The purpose of the Church is ministry (service) which must operate in Gods' government which is kingdom of heaven divine order. We all have that purpose and destiny to fulfill. Destiny is the place where you and I will end up spending eternity Jesus explain it this way:
Enter you in at the straight gate: for wide is the gate, and broad is the way, that lead to destruction and many there be which go in there. Because straight is the gate, and narrow is the way, which lead unto life, and few there be that find it.
Gods' government is not of this world his kingdom is about soul winning to bring everyone that is to come into the kingdom When Jesus told Peter I will make you fisher of men, but there was a condition that he had to follow he said follow me. The Lord told his disciples if they follow him, they would be successful in the kingdom. For the Kingdom of God is not meat drink, but righteousness, joy and, peace in the Holy Ghost.

Romans 14:17

Prayer Watchers of the Lord

I know there is a certain time of morning the Lord wakes' you up to prayer, if you don't know your purpose for waking up for prayer early morning obey him it is the Lord directing you to get up and pray!
First Prayer watch-6p.m.-12 midnight
Second Prayer watch- 9 a.m.-12 noon
Third Prayer watch- 12 midnight 3.am.
Fourth Prayer- watch 3 a.m.-6 a.m.
Fifth Prayer -watch -6 a.m.-9 a.m.
Six Prayer watch- 9a.m.-12 noon
Seventh Prayer watch-3 p.m.- 6p.m
During the watch, pray along these lines:
Time to pray and silence all the voices (curses) of the enemies on your life, family, church,

city and nation. Witches start flying during this watch, going around the precincts of the city Psalms 59 because they intend to take hold of the gates of the day. We must possess the gate of our new day. Otherwise, it will be the enemies possessing them, releasing curses on our day. It is the time to release judgement on the wicked, because this is the time, we have the evening tide in line with Isaiah 17:12-14.

1. Covenant Renewal with God. It was the watch during which Jesus broke bread with his covenant between God and Israel. It is the time to appropriate the provisions in the Blood Covenant. Every covenant you have with god can be renewed at this time.

2. Time for the nature of the Lamb of god. The ability to do what others can't do: Behold the Lamb, the lion of the tribe of Judah who is able to break every yoke and the seals the title deed of the universal (power, wealth, strength, wisdom, honor, glory and blessing) Humility is the greatest secret of his strength: that is the reason why during this watch, he tied the towel around his waist and washed his disciple's feet leadership is service.

3. Time for Preservation of the fruits of life especially the fruits of the body. Every executive/leader can begin to pray for every project he starts to live out its divinely ordained lifespan.

Second Watch

1. Time of Harvest Acts 2:41 Promises, this is the time to expect the manifestation of Gods' promises for your life as in
2. Time for Blessing
3. The blessing of the Lord makes you rich
4. Bless the lord O my soul
5. The case of David in 2 Samuel 7:25-29
6. Time to pray and appropriate the benefits of the Cross.

Healing, prosperity, forgiveness, strength, etc.

Jesus was crucified at the third hour Mark 15:25, Matt. 27:45 After having been on the cross for three hours, darkness came upon the face on the earth at 12 noon, and then at 3:00 P.M., the period of darkness ended.

7. Pray for a crucified life because his crucified let us ask god to help is manifest all the values of crucified life, by mortifying the deeds of the flesh as stated in Romans 8:12-15. This is the time to cut out the old man and put on the new man the Lord Jesus Christ. Col. 3:2-11. This is the time to nail witchcraft, bitterness, jealousy, anger, backbiting, gossip, slander, lying, deception, hypocrisy and the fact all properties and personality traits of the devil and all the works of the flesh nail to the cross. Gal. 2:20, 5:19-21.

8. Pray for forgiveness, healing of Relationships, Pray for release

of others. Forgive us our trespasses as we forgive. This is the be time to pray this portion of prayer.

Third Watch

Time for spiritual warfare, this is third of the night and one of the important. Overruling human decrees. Exodus 12-14. This is when the deep sleep fall upon men according to Acts 20:7-12. And while men slept the enemy went to sow. This is a period of heightened satanic activities. This is the time rapist increases their activity, according to judges 19, pray to silences them.

Time of release from prison Isa. 42:22 Jude 16:3. This is time to pray to god and make your case in prayer, also pray for every emergency provision God makes to be released Luke 11:5-13 this is the time for most dream Job 4:13-14; time for miracles or covenants; time for apply the blood of Jesus the time to confront every storm of destruction and distraction time to speak peace into every situation of turbulence and confusion.

Fourth Prayer Watch

This watch ushers in and begins at this hour of prayer according to Acts 3:1, Acts 10:30, Isa 60-11:23, this one single most important characteristic or practice that identifies the church is Prayer the important privilege the entire church is prayer and the only how in the bible that is specifically referred to as the hour of prayer begins at 3:00 p.m. This was the time that the veil in front of the Holy of Holies tore from top to bottom. This watch is therefore the time access.

1.   The hour of prayer, covenant and, power and triumph glory time to remove limiting. This is the establishment of the Kingdom, Why? Righteousness and Justice are the foundation of his Throne. At this hour Jesus said, it is finished. At 3.00 p.m. Jesus gave up the ghost. Jesus went through six hours of suffering for the deliverance of human kind and the universe. It is also the hour for miraculous and angelic visitation. Zech. 1:10-11, 18-21.

2.   Time to change /shape of history, this was the time God changed history because this watch.

3.   Time to pray for the gate of the day. just like in other watches not only for yourself but also for your family, for villages, your neighborhood, your community, the city, the nations, and the church of Gods' Kingdom.

Fifty Watch

The outpouring of the Holy Ghost- Acts 2,4, 17,18

The Holy Spirit came before the third hour, this is the first watch of the day the watch for the beginning to sunrise. Six Prayer Watch- Time for Harvest -Acts 2:41 Promise, this is the time to expect the manifestation of God's promises for your life as in the case David *2 Samuel 7:25-29* Also appropriate the promises for cleaning, a new heart, willingness to; work increase and fruitfulness, as contained in. *Ez. 36:25-38.*

    a.   Time to pray and appropriate the benefits of the cross

    b.   Pray for forgiveness.

    c.   Pray for healing.

    d.   Pray for healing and diseases.

Seven prayer Watch

1. Time to be in Secret Place of the Most –
2. High for Protection. Psalms 91:1.
3. Pray for the Church
4. Pray for the Nation
5. Pray for common election
6. Pray to change the media landscape.

Eight Prayer Watch

Prayer God will baptize every Christian with hatred for sin in our generation.

Ask the Lord to remove every obstacle and hinderance. Pray God will redeem our spiritual sight from all the things that have blinded us from seeing vision of God.

Now is the time to sum up all your experience and pain, not only do he use your experiences he also us your pain. I heard a minister without pain in your experience there is no growth. No pain no gain in your spiritual development, as you read the book of Habakkuk God tell the prophet to write the vision make it plain, he will make your feet like hinds' feet to walk in high places. Our journey to the place call there is a journey of suffering and much pain if we are following Christ It is your way to become mature in him it will not be a piece of cake, but if you will learn valuable lessons on that road because after all you have done to stand and see what the end will be you will begin to see more clearly that you are growing, and not staying in one place.

He needs you to grow up in him I remember when I was a babe in Christ at that level everything I asked God for I received it. When it was time for me to stop crawling and start walking thought I wasn't saved anymore you see no one taught me or took me under the wings, so I backslide. We are not meant to remain as children but to grow up in every way into Christ I did not realize that God wanted me to grow up had not heard such thing. But what I see in the body of Christ now are developmental disabilities; also known an immature spiritually. It is a thing, because I have a daughter who is developmental delayed, so I understand and see the symptoms in the body of Christ. Here is the kicker even though I backslide a few times after so many times you will have to decide before God gives you up. He will let you go on your way if you keep rejecting him. I was no different than the prodigal son on my way to a place of torment but, he had mercy on my soul. Do you know there are so many people who chances ran out? I am so thankful to be able to share my testimonies, my experiences, my pain and struggles with others. I feel in the spirit someone else is going through you need to know that you are not the only one. Know that all things work together for your good let him make you over no pain, no gain.

Ephesians 4:1

Therefore, the prisoner of the lord; beseech you that you that walk worthy of the vocation wherewith you are called, with all lowliness and meekness, with long suffering, forbearing one another in love; Endeavoring to keep the unity of Spirit in the bond of peace. There is one body and one Spirit even as you are called in one hope of your calling; one Lord, one faith one baptism one God and Father of all, who is above all and every one of us is given grace according to the measure of the gift of Christ.

I say, thank you Jesus for allowing me to return to the fold with right mind, and right attitude, and willingness to learn all that I missed and still become who you call me to be I never would have made it without you. it was by your grace alone. I had no clue that I was a writer, author this I never dreamed or the thought I come to me. I thought I thought I was to be doing something else this is like a dream that could not be attained I only captured this in being obedient unto Jesus. If you think this is something already knew how to do I want you to know, I had no idea how to write or publish. Therefore, you can't quit no matter how much pain and suffering you go through. If the suffer with him is to reign and rule with him. I write from my struggle my experience, my pain we are overcomers by the blood of the Lamb.

Ephesians 4:11-16

He gave some to be apostles; and some prophets; and some evangelists; and some, pastors, and teachers; for the perfecting of the saints, to the work of the ministry, to the building up of the body of Christ; until we all come into the unity of the faith, and knowledge of the son of God, to a full grown man, to the measure of stature of the fullness of Christ; that we may no longer be children , tossed back and forth and carried about with every wind of doctrine, by the ticks of men and craftiness after the wiles of error; but speaking truth in love, may grow up in all things into him who is the head Christ; from whom all the body being fitted and knit together through that which every joint supplies according to the working in measure of each individual part, makes the body increase to the building up of itself in love.

The Gospel of Jesus Christ is about turning the sinner into disciples of God who will follow Jesus Christ in holiness and righteousness and serve the Kingdom of god. True Children of God do not be distracted those are the one who will be save in the end. One is not derailed to deceived these are the true children of God.

Matthew 28:19-

Go ye therefore and teach all nations. This is the great commission Jesus gave the church to go into all the world to preach the Gospel the reason this commission is to go into the world the scripture declares that Satan is the god of this world. 2 Corinthians 4:4. In other words Satan have blinded the mind of those who do not believe in the world.

The gospel message is needed it might be a place where you work. Going to fellow workers is going into the world. The system in the world maybe the school system. We do not have to move to the other side of the world to preach the Gospel. The mission field could be right down the street or on the other side of the city in a neighborhood where the culture and customs are different than your own.

Prophecy to us Smooth Things

Isaiah 30:10

They say to the seers, do not see to those who have visions, do not tell us vision you have as they really are but flatter us, Prophecy deceit.

There are those who take the gift of prophecy, and use it to dictate, control to guide others life. The people in Isaiah's day once again just because a believer has the gift of prophecy don't mean one is a Prophet. Now I am not against prophesying, or Prophets it is time to come out of the religion and tradition mindset. It is time to pulldown strongholds and embrace the truth. The day of the turn- around for hearing about new cars, money, housing, husbands are over God is in the blessing business; but his promises are yea and amen. I love prophesying lets' face it if we are just wanting things from God and not seeking his face, his presence the motive of our heart, are wrong. We will be held accountable for having truth and telling lies deceiving.

Jeremiah 14:14

Then the Lord said unto me the Prophets prophesy lies in my name I sent them not neither appointed them or spoken to them. They are prophesying to you false vision, divination, idolatry and the delusion of their hearts.

Telling lies, saying things coming from their own mind false things and some even build their ministry or church upon prophesying and people flock to this sometimes even me, because when the Lord send me someone where I just flow with the ministry you just can't go into another mans' house and tell him how to run his house. I visit different churches I love varieties God like varieties there are not many real ministries around but there are a few. You will suffer persecution for the Gospel of Jesus Christ be prepared for it. This faith , love walk is not a piece of cake we are watched by a great of cloud of witnesses let us lay aside every weight and sin which so easily beset us and let us run this race with patient looking to Jesus the author and finisher of our faith; who endured the cross, despising the shame, and is set down at the right of the throne of God.

Frederick Douglas
Abolitionist, Orator, Journalist

Born in 1817 in Cordova, Md; a central figure in the campaign to abolish slavery, he established the newspaper North Star and issued it for 17 years: advisor to Harriet Beecher Stowe and President Abraham Lincoln: Unite States minister to Haiti: author of several books: died is 1895.

I was not more than thirteen years old, when in my loneliness and destitution I longed for someone one to whom I could go, as to a father and protector. The preaching of a white Methodist minister, named Hanson, was the means of causing me to feel that in god I had such a friend. He thought that all men, great and small, bond and free, were sinners in the sight of God: that they were by nature rebels against his government; and that they must repent of their sins and be reconciled to God through Christ. I cannot say that I had a very distinct notion of what was required of me, but one thing I did know well: I was wretched and had no means of making myself otherwise. I consulted a good colored man named Charles Lawson, and in tones of holy affection he told me to pray, and to cast all my cares upon God." This I sought to do; and though for weeks I was a poor, brokenhearted mourner, traveling through doubts and fears, I finally found my burden lightened, and my heart reveled I loved all mankind, slaveholders not excepted, though I abhorred slavery more than ever I saw the world in a new light, and my great concern was to have everybody converted. My desire to learn increased, and especially did I want a thorough acquaintance with them.

Mary McLeod Bethune, Educator:

Born in 1875 Maysville, S. C.; educated at Scotia Seminary and Moody Bible Institute; founded Bethune-Cookman college, 1924: President of the school until 1942; Spingarn Medal1935; Francis A Drexel Award, 1936; Thomas Jefferson Award, 1942; Haitian Medal of Honor, 1949; received several honorary degrees; founder and President , National Council of Negro Women; special advisor to President franklin Roosevelt; named" Mother of the Century" by the Dorie Miller foundation, 1954; died in 1955.

Sometimes we get too proud to acknowledge our religious background of simple, pious Christian faith. It is strange that made us what we are as a people!

I am greatly concerned with the fact that as the standards of education are being raised, there is somehow less and less emphasis on the teaching of the Word.

Secularization is a process that sets in when a society becomes proud, but God confounds such.

How can any man call himself educated who has knowledge of the Bible in the hands and in the hearts of its people?

Perhaps we don't know the God of the bible, or our Father and creator to whom we owe life itself the bible is our means of such acquaintance, and through it every man is free to form his own friendship with the divine.

Chicago Defender, October 9, 1954

Martin Luther King, Jr.

Clergy Civil Rights Leader

Born in 1920 at Atlanta, Ga.; educated at More House College, Crozier Theological Seminary, and Boston University; received several honorary degrees; president Southern Christian Leadership Cong.; Time Magazine Man of the year" for 1963; Nobel Peace Prize, 1964; Nehru Award, 1966; author of several books died in 1968.

I would urge you to give priority the search for God allow his Spirit to permeate your being. To meet the difficulties and challenges of life you will need him before the ship of your life researches its last harbor the ship of your life researches its last harbor, there will long, drawn-out storms, howling and jostling winds, and tempestuous seas that make seas that make the heart stand still. If you do not have a deep and patient faith in God, you will be powerless to face the delays, disappointments, and vicissitudes that inevitably come. Without God, all our efforts turn to ashes and our sunrises into darkest night. Without him, life is a meaningless drama in which the decisive scenes are missing, but with him, we can rise from tension-packed valleys to the sublime heights of inner peace to find radiant stars of hope against the nocturnal bosom of life's most depressing nights. St. Augustine was right: Thou has created us for thyself, and our heart con not be quieted till it find response in thee.

About the Author

Deborah is a writer, author, publisher, teacher of the scriptures, God gives her dream and vision she operates in interpretation of dreams and visions. God gives her revelation concern the Kingdom of Heaven: Deborah has written –

The Mystery of the Kingdom through Dreams, Visions and the Word, The Interpretations of Dreams, Exposing false Prophets, Teachers, and Doctrines.

If you want to check out her books you can also get the e-book to your phone @ amazon.com @ Barnes & nobles.com

We walk by faith and not by sight.

You can contact Deborah by email @:
Deborah58dee53@gmail.com
Website coming soon

About the Author

Deborah is a southern girl born in Shreveport Louisiana to the parents of Clifford Edward Jones and Vernell Jones Drew coming from southern hospitality to the big city of Dallas where she now lives. On her Journey in the Kingdom of light years of church frustration, and backsliding, rejection, merry go round, burn out church going Deborah finally had enough of religion and tradition of the same setting every year in christendom. God are you there? Are you real? Is this all to life? Seeking out these questions not only did she find a personal relationship with him she also found her identity in him. God is raising up a militant people and he is bringing them in as the Holy Spirit teach them who they are as a student of the Word the Holy Spirit will take you on a joyous adventure you have never dreamed.

Deborah flow in the anointing of:

Dreams, Visions, and Revelation of the Word of God, exposing the tactic of the enemy. Sher is an author writer, publisher in her baby stage but after the lessons bought she is learning first had if you want it done right learn it yourself. Coming into what she calls a paradigm shift from religion to the true lifestyle of holiness with Jesus being the author and finisher of her faith.

Prophecy to us Smooth Things
Isaiah 30:10

They say the seers, do not see to those who have visions, do not tell us vision you have as they really are but flatter us, Prophesy deceit.

There are those who take the gift of prophecy, and use it to dictate, control to guide others life. The people in Isaiah day did not want to hear the truth they want to hear lies and deceit from the prophets. If you are a true prophet this does not apply you, I have had my share so don't be offended. I am not against prophets or prophesying, but I am for truth and not deception and mind control we have enough that from so call pimps in the world. It is time to pulldown strongholds, so we can embrace the truth the day for turn- around is now. The promises of God are yea and amen stop dipping into your neighbors' well and find your inheritance in the kingdom. All believers have an inheritance in the kingdom spiritually first then physically. Stop being lazy seek it out for yourself!

Prophesy Smooth things people with the tickle ears.

A PLACE CALL THERE IS A WORD GOD GAVE ME MANY YEARS AGO BACK IN THE NINETIES WHEN MY GRANDSON DAMARCUS WAYNE JONES WAS ALIVE. Damarcus was born on October28, 1995- February,22- 2013.

IN LOVING MEMORY OF MY GRANDSON:
DAMARCUS WAYNE JONES- R.I.P.

www.ingramcontent.com/pod-product-compliance
Lightning Source LLC
Chambersburg PA
CBHW041208100726
47911CB00017B/896